R-6

J

876-363

Asimov — David Starr: Space ranger

David Starr: Space Ranger

THE LUCKY STARR SERIES
by Isaac Asimov

David Starr:
Space Ranger

by Isaac Asimov

Twayne Publishers • Boston, Massachusetts • 1978

This edition published in 1978 by Gregg Press
A Division of G. K. Hall & Co.
by arrangement with Doubleday & Co., Inc.
and with the cooperation of Isaac Asimov

Jacket and frontmatter art by Wayne Barlowe
Jacket and fontmatter design by John Balta

Printed on permanent/durable acid-free paper and bound
in the United States of America

First Printing, October 1978

Library of Congress Cataloging in Publication Data

Asimov, Isaac, 1920–
David Starr, space ranger.

(The Lucky Starr series)
Reprint of the 1st ed. published by Doubleday,
Garden City, N.Y.
I. Title. II. Series.
[PZ3.A8316Dav 1978] [PS3551.S5] 813'.5'4
ISBN 0-8398-2486-6   78-14573

PREFACE

Back in the 1950s, I wrote a series of six derring-do novels about David "Lucky" Starr and his battles against malefactors within the Solar System. Each of the six took place in a different region of the system, and in each case I made use of the astronomical facts—as they were then known.

Now, a quarter-century later, Gregg Press is bringing out the novels in new hardcover editions; but what a quarter-century it has been! More has been learned about the worlds of our Solar System in this last quarter-century than in all the thousands of years that went before.

DAVID STARR: SPACE RANGER was written in 1951 and at that time, there was still a faint possibility that there were canals on Mars, as had first been reported three-quarters of a century earlier. There was, therefore, a faint possibility that intelligent life existed there, or had existed at one time.

Since then, though, we have sent probes past Mars and around it to take photographs of its surface, and map the entire planet. In 1976, we even landed small laboratories on the Martian surface to test its soil.

There are no canals. There are instead, craters, giant volcanoes and enormous canyons. The atmosphere is only 1 percent as dense as Earth's and is almost entirely carbon dioxide. There is no clear sign of any life at all upon Mars, and the possibility of advanced life upon it, now or ever, seems nil.

If I had written the book today, I would have had to adjust the plot to take all this into account.

I hope my Gentle Readers enjoy the book anyway, as an adventure story, but please don't forget that the advance of science can outdate even the most conscientious science-fiction writer and that my astronomical descriptions are no longer accurate in all respects.

ISAAC ASIMOV

★ ★ ★ ★ Dedication

To WALTER I. BRADBURY,

without whom this book

would *really*

never have been written

★★★★ CONTENTS

★★★★DAVID STARR

space ranger

★ ★ ★ ★ Chapter 1

THE PLUM FROM MARS

David Starr was staring right at the man, so he saw it happen. He saw him die.

David had been waiting patiently for Dr. Henree and, in the meanwhile, enjoying the atmosphere of International City's newest restaurant. This was to be his first real celebration now that he had obtained his degree and qualified for full membership in the Council of Science.

He did not mind waiting. The Café Supreme still glistened from the freshly applied chromosilicone paints. The subdued light that spread evenly over the entire dining room had no visible source. At the wall end of David's table was the small, self-glowing cube which contained a tiny three-dimensional replica of the band whose music filled in a soft background. The leader's baton was a half-inch flash of motion and of course the table top itself was of the Sanito type, the ultimate in force-field modernity and, except for the deliberate flicker, quite invisible.

David's calm brown eyes swept the other tables, half-hidden in their alcoves, not out of boredom, but because people interested him more than any of the scientific gadgetry that the Café Supreme could gather. Tri-television and force-fields were wonders ten years before, yet were already accepted by all. People, on the other hand, did not change, but even now, ten thousand years after the pyramids were built and five thousand years after the first atom bomb had exploded, they were still the insoluble mystery and the unfaded wonder.

There was a young girl in a pretty gown laughing gently with the man who sat opposite her; a middle-aged man, in uncomfortable holiday clothing, punching the menu combination on the mechanical waiter while his wife and two children watched gravely; two business-men talking animatedly over their dessert.

And it was as David's glance flicked over the business-men that it happened. One of them, face congesting with blood, moved convulsively and attempted to rise. The other, crying out, stretched out an arm in a vague gesture of help, but the first had already collapsed in his seat and was beginning to slide under the table.

David had risen to his feet at the first sign of disturbance and now his long legs ate the distance between the tables in three quick strides. He was in the booth and, at a touch of his finger on the electronic contact near the tri-television cube, a violet curtain with fluorescent designs swept across the open end of the alcove. It would attract no attention. Many diners preferred to take advantage of that sort of privacy.

The sick man's companion only now found his voice. He said, "Manning is ill. It's some sort of seizure. Are you a doctor?"

David's voice was calm and level. It carried assurance. He said, "Now sit quietly and make no noise. We will have the manager here and what can be done will be done."

He had his hands on the sick man, lifting him as though he were a rag doll, although the man was heavy-set. He pushed the table as far to one side as possible, his fingers separated uncannily by an inch of force-field as he gripped it. He laid the man on the seat, loosening the Magno-seams of his blouse, and began applying artificial respiration.

David had no illusion as to the possibility of recovery. He knew the symptoms: the sudden flushing, the loss of voice and breath, the few minutes' fight for life, and then, the end.

The curtain brushed aside. With admirable dispatch the manager had answered the emergency signal which David had tapped even before he had left his own table. The manager was a short, plump man, dressed in black, tightly fitting clothing of conservative cut. His face was disturbed.

"Did someone in this wing——" He seemed to shrink in upon himself as his eyes took in the sight.

The surviving diner was speaking with hysterical

rapidity. "We were having dinner when my friend had this seizure. As for this other man, I don't know who he is."

David abandoned his futile attempts at revival. He brushed his thick brown hair off his forehead. He said, "You are the manager?"

"I am Oliver Gaspere, manager of the Café Supreme," said the plump man bewilderedly. "The emergency call from Table 87 sounds and when I come, it is empty. I am told a young man has just run into the booth of Table 94, and I follow and find this." He turned. "I shall call the house doctor."

David said, "One moment. There is no use in that. This man is dead."

"What!" cried the other diner. He lunged forward, crying, "Manning!"

David Starr pulled him back, pinning him against the unseeable table top. "Easy, man. You cannot help him and this is no time for noise."

"No, no," Gaspere agreed rapidly. "We must not up-set the other diners. But see here, sir, a doctor must still examine this poor man to decide the cause of death. I can allow no irregularities in my restaurant."

"I am sorry, Mr. Gaspere, but I forbid the examina-tion of this man by anyone at the moment."

"What are you talking about? If this man dies of a heart attack——"

"Please. Let us have co-operation and not useless dis-cussion. What is your name, sir?"

The living diner said dully, "Eugene Forester."

"Well, then, Mr. Forester, I want to know exactly what you and your companion ate just now."

"Sir!" The little manager stared at David, with eyes swelling out of their sockets. "Are you suggesting that something in the food caused this?"

"I'm not making suggestions. I'm asking questions."

"You have no right to ask questions. Who are you? You are nobody. I demand that a doctor examine this poor man."

"Mr. Gaspere, this is Council of Science business."

David bared the inner surface of his wrist, curling the flexible Metallite sleeve above it. For a moment it was merely exposed skin, and then an oval spot darkened and turned black. Within it little yellow grains of light danced and flickered in the familiar patterns of the Big Dipper and of Orion.

The manager's lips trembled. The Council of Science was not an official government agency, but its members were nearly above the government.

He said, "I am sorry, sir."

"No apologies are necessary. Now, Mr. Forester, will you answer my first question?"

Forester muttered, "We had the special dinner number three."

"Both of you?"

"That's right."

David said, "Were there no substitutions on either part?" He had studied the menu at his own table. The Café Supreme featured extraterrestrial delicacies, but the special dinner number three was one of the more ordinary meals native to Earth: vegetable soup, veal chops, baked potato, peas, ice cream, and coffee.

"Yes, there *was* a substitution." Forester's brows drew together. "Manning ordered stewed marplums for dessert."

"And you didn't?"

"No."

"And where are the marplums now?" David had eaten them himself. They were plums grown in the vast Martian greenhouses, juicy and pitless, with a faint cinnamon flavor superimposed on their fruitiness.

Forester said, "He ate them. What do you suppose?"

"How soon before he collapsed?"

"About five minutes, I think. We hadn't even finished our coffee." The man was turning sickly pale. "Were they poisoned?"

David did not answer. He turned to the manager. "What about the marplums?"

"There was nothing wrong with them. Nothing." Gaspere seized the curtains of the alcove and shook them in his passion, but did not forget to speak in the softest of whispers. "They were a fresh shipment from Mars, government tested and approved. We have served hundreds of portions in the last three nights alone. Nothing like this has happened till now."

"Just the same you had better give orders to eliminate marplums from the list of desserts until we can inspect them again. And now, in case it wasn't the marplums at all, please bring me a carton of some sort and we will transfer what is left of the dinner for study."

16

"Immediately. Immediately."

"And of course speak to no one of this."

The manager returned in a few moments, smearing his brow with a feathery handkerchief. He said, "I cannot understand it. I really cannot."

David stowed the used plastic dishes, with scraps of food still adhering to them, in the carton, added what was left of the toasted rolls, recapped the waxed cups in which the coffee had been served, and put them aside. Gaspere left off rubbing his hands frantically to reach a finger toward the contact at the edge of the table.

David's hand moved quickly, and the manager was startled to find his wrist imprisoned.

"But, sir, the crumbs!"

"I'll take those too." He used his penknife to collect each scrap, its sharp steel sliding easily along the nothingness of the force-field. David himself doubted the worth of force-field table tops. Their sheer transparency was anything but conducive to relaxation. The sight of dishes and cutlery resting on nothing could not help but leave diners tense, so that the field had to be put deliberately out of phase to induce continual interference sparkles that gave rise to an illusion of substance.

In restaurants they were popular since at the conclusion of a meal it was necessary only to extend the force-field a fraction of an inch to destroy whatever adhering crumbs and drops remained. It was only when David had concluded his collection that he allowed Gaspere to perform the extension, removing the safety catch first by a touch of the finger and then permitting

Gaspere to use his special key. A new, absolutely clean surface was instantly presented.

"And now, just a moment." David glanced at the metal face of his wrist watch, then flicked a corner of the curtain aside.

He said softly, "Dr. Henree!"

The lanky middle-aged man who was sitting on what had been David's seat fifteen minutes earlier stiffened and looked about him with surprise.

David was smiling. "Here I am!" He put a finger to his lips.

Dr. Henree rose. His clothes hung loosely upon him and his thinning gray hair was combed carefully over a bald spot. He said, "My dear David, are you here already? I had thought you were late. But is anything wrong?"

David's smile had been short-lived. He said, "It's another one."

Dr. Henree stepped within the curtain, looked at the dead man, and muttered, "Dear me."

"That's one way of putting it," said David.

"I think," said Dr. Henree, removing his glasses and playing the mild force-beam of his pencil-cleaner over the lenses before replacing them, "I think we had better close down the restaurant."

Gaspere opened and closed his mouth soundlessly, like a fish. Finally he said in a strangled gasp, "Close the restaurant! It has been open only a week. It will be ruin. Absolute ruin!"

"Oh, but only for an hour or so. We will have to remove the body and inspect your kitchens. Surely you want us to remove the stigma of food poisoning if we can, and surely it would be even less convenient for you to have us make arrangements for this in the presence of the diners."

"Very well then. I will see that the restaurant is made available to you, but I must have an hour's grace to allow present diners to finish their meals. I hope there will be no publicity."

"None, I assure you." Dr. Henree's lined face was a mask of worry. "David, will you call Council Hall and ask to speak to Conway? We have a procedure for such cases. He will know what to do."

"Must I stay?" put in Forester suddenly. "I feel sick."

"Who is this, David?" asked Dr. Henree.

"The dead man's dinner companion. His name is Forester."

"Oh. Then I am afraid, Mr. Forester, you will have to be sick here."

The restaurant was cold and repulsive in its emptiness. Silent operatives had come and gone. Efficiently they had gone through the kitchens atom by atom. Now only Dr. Henree and David Starr remained. They sat in an empty alcove. There were no lights, and the tri-tele-visions on each table were simply dead cubes of glass.

Dr. Henree shook his head. "We will learn nothing. I am sure of that from experience. I am sorry, David. This is not the proper celebration we had planned."

"Plenty of time for celebration later. You mentioned

in your letters these cases of food poisoning, so I was pre-pared. Still, I wasn't aware of this intense secrecy which seems necessary. I might have been more discreet if I had known."

"No. It is no use. We cannot hide this trouble forever. Little by little there are tiny leaks. People see other people die while eating and then hear of still other cases. Always while they're eating. It is bad and will grow worse. Well, we will talk more of this tomorrow when you talk to Conway himself."

"Wait!" David looked deep into the older man's eyes. "There is something that worries you more than the death of a man or the death of a thousand. Something I don't know. What is it?"

Dr. Henree sighed. "I'm afraid, David, that Earth is in great danger. Most of the Council does not believe it and Conway is only half-convinced, but I am certain that this supposed food poisoning is a clever and brutal attempt at seizing control of Earth's economic life and government. And so far, David, there is no hint as to who is behind the threat and exactly how it is being accomplished. The Council of Science is entirely helpless!"

★ ★ ★ ★ Chapter 2

THE BREADBASKET IN THE SKY

Hector Conway, Chief Counselor of Science, stood at his window in the topmost suite of Science Tower, the slender structure which dominated the northern suburbs of International City. The city was beginning to sparkle in the early twilight. Soon it would turn to streaks of white along the elevated pedestrian promenades. The buildings would light up in jeweled patterns as the windows came to life. Almost centered in his window were the distant domes of the Halls of Congress, with the Executive Mansion snuggled between.

He was alone in his office, and the automatic lock was adjusted to Dr. Henree's fingerprints only. He could feel some of his depression lifting. David Starr was on his way, suddenly and magically grown up, ready to receive his first assignment as a member of the Council. He felt almost as though his son were about to visit him. In a way, that was how it was. David Starr *was* his son: his and Augustus Henree's.

There had been three of them at first, himself and Gus Henree and Lawrence Starr. How he remembered Lawrence Starr! They had all three gone through school together, qualified for the Council together, done their first investigations together; and then Lawrence Starr had been promoted. It was to be expected; he was by far the most brilliant of the three.

So he had received a semi-permanent station on Venus, and that was the first time the three had not tackled a proposition together. He had gone with his wife and child. The wife was Barbara. Lovely Barbara Starr! Neither Henree nor himself had ever married, and for neither were there any girls to compete with Barbara in memory. When David was born, it was Uncle Gus and Uncle Hector, until he sometimes got confused and called his father Uncle Lawrence.

And then on the trip to Venus there was the pirate attack. It had been a total massacre. Pirate ships took virtually no prisoners in space, and more than a hundred human beings were dead before two hours had passed. Among them were Lawrence and Barbara.

Conway could remember the day, the exact minute, when the news had reached Science Tower. Patrol ships had shot out into space, tracing the pirates; they attacked the asteroid lairs in a fury that was completely unprecedented. Whether they caught the particular villains who had gutted the Venus-bound ship none could ever say, but the pirate power had been broken from that year on.

And the patrol ships found something else: a tiny lifeboat winding a precarious orbit between Venus and Earth, radiating its coldly automatic radio calls for help. Only a child was inside. A frightened, lonely four-year-old, who did not speak for hours except to say stoutly, "Mother said I wasn't to cry."

It was David Starr. His story, seen through childish eyes, was garbled, but interpretation was only too easy. Conway could still see what those last minutes within the gutted ship must have been like: Lawrence Starr, dying in the control room, with the outlaws forcing their way in; Barbara, a blast gun in her hand, desperately thrusting David into the lifeboat, trying to set the controls as best she could, rocketing it into space. And then?

She had a gun in her hand. As long as she could, she must have used it against the enemy, and when that could be no longer, against herself.

Conway ached to think of it. Ached, and once again wished they had allowed him to accompany the patrol ships so that with his own hands he might have helped to turn the asteroid caves into flaming oceans of atomic destruction. But members of the Council of Science, they said, were too valuable to risk in police actions, so he stayed home and read the news bulletins as they rolled out on the ticker tape of his telenews projector.

Between them he and Augustus Henree had adopted David Starr, bent their lives to erase those last horrible memories of space. They were both mother and father to him; they personally supervised his tutoring; they trained him with one thought in mind: to make him what Lawrence Starr had once been.

He had exceeded their expectations. In height he was Lawrence, reaching six feet, rangy and hard, with the cool nerves and quick muscles of an athlete and the sharp, clear brain of a first-class scientist. And beyond that there was something about his brown hair with the suggestion of a wave in it, in his level, wide-set brown eyes, in the trace of a cleft in his chin which vanished when he smiled, that was reminiscent of Barbara.

He had raced through his Academy days leaving a trail of sparks and the dead ash of previous records both on the playing fields and in the classrooms.

Conway had been perturbed. "It's not natural, Gus. He's outdoing his father."

And Henree, who didn't believe in unnecessary speech, had puffed at his pipe and smiled proudly.

"I hate to say this," Conway had continued, "because you'll laugh at me, but there's something not quite normal in it. Remember that the child was stranded in space for two days with just a thin lifeboat hull between himself and solar radiation. He was only seventy million miles from the sun during a period of sunspot maximum."

"All you're saying," said Henree, "is that David should have been burnt to death."

"Well, I don't know," mumbled Conway. "The effect of radiation on living tissue, on *human* living tissue, has its mysteries."

"Well, naturally. It's not a field in which experimentation is very feasible."

David had finished college with the highest average on record. He had managed to do original work in biophysics on the graduate level. He was the youngest man ever to be accorded full membership in the Council of Science.

To Conway there had been a loss in all this. Four years earlier he had been elected Chief Counselor. It was an honor he would have given his life for, yet he knew that had Lawrence Starr lived, the election would have gone in a worthier direction.

And he had lost all but occasional contact with young David Starr, for to be Chief Counselor meant that one had no life other than the beetling problems of all the Galaxy. Even at graduation exercises he had seen David only from a distance. In the last four years he might have spoken to him four times.

So his heart beat high when he heard the door open. He turned, walking rapidly to meet them as they walked in.

"Gus old man." He held out his hand, wrung the other's. "And David boy!"

An hour passed. It was true night before they could stop speaking of themselves and turn to the universe.

It was David who broke out. He said, "I saw my first poisoning today, Uncle Hector. I knew enough to prevent panic. I wish I knew enough to prevent poisoning."

Conway said soberly, "No one knows that much. I suppose, Gus, it was a Martian product again."

"No way of telling, Hector. But a marplum was involved."

"Suppose," said David Starr, "you let me know anything I'm allowed to know about this."

"It's remarkably simple," said Conway. "Horribly simple. In the last four months something like two hundred people have died immediately after eating some Mars-grown product. It's no known poison, the symptoms are those of no known disease. There is a rapid and complete paralysis of the nerves controlling the diaphragm and the muscles of the chest. It amounts to a paralysis of the lungs, which is fatal in five minutes.

"It goes deeper than that too. In the few cases where we've caught the victims in time, we've tried artificial respiration, as you did, and even iron lungs. They still died in five minutes. The heart is affected as well. Autopsies show us nothing except nerve degeneration that must have been unbelievably rapid."

"What about the food that poisoned them?" asked David.

"Dead end," said Conway. "There is always time for the poisoned item or portion to be completely consumed. Other specimens of the same sort at the table or in the kitchen are harmless. We've fed them to animals and even to human volunteers. The stomach contents of the dead men have yielded uncertain results."

"Then how do you know it's food poisoning at all?"

"Because the coincidence of death after eating a Martian product time after time, without known exception, is more than coincidence."

David said thoughtfully, "And it isn't contagious, obviously."

"No. Thank the stars for that. Even so, it's bad enough. So far we've kept this as quiet as we can, with full co-operation from the Planetary Police. Two hundred deaths in four months over the population of all Earth is still a manageable phenomenon, but the rate may increase. And if the people of Earth become aware that any mouthful of Martian food might be their last, the consequences could be horrible. Even though we were to point out that the death rate is only fifty per month out of a population of five billions, each person would think himself certain to be one of those fifty."

"Yes," said David, "and that would mean that the market for Martian food imports would fall through the floor. It would be too bad for the Martian Farming Syndicates."

"That!" Conway shrugged his shoulders, thrusting aside the problem of the Farming Syndicates as something of no moment. "Do you see nothing else?"

"I see that Earth's own agriculture can't support five billion people."

"That's it exactly. We can't do without food from the colonial planets. There would be starvation on Earth in six weeks. Yet if the people are afraid of Martian food, there will be no preventing that, and I don't know how long it can be staved off. Each new death is a new crisis.

Will this be the one that the telenews will get hold of? Will the truth come out now? And there's Gus's theory on top of everything."

Dr. Henree sat back, tamping tobacco gently into his pipe. "I feel sure, David, that this epidemic of food poisoning is not a natural phenomenon. It is too widespread. It strikes one day in Bengal, the next day in New York, the day after in Zanzibar. There must be intelligence behind it."

"I tell you——" began Conway.

"Let him go on, Uncle Hector," urged David.

"If any group were seeking to control Earth, what better move could they make than to strike at our weakest point, our food supply? Earth is the most populous planet in all the Galaxy. It should be, since it is mankind's original home. But that very fact makes us the weakest world, in a sense, since we're not self-supporting. Our breadbasket is in the sky: on Mars; on Ganymede; on Europa. If you cut the imports in any manner, either by pirate action or by the much more subtle system being used now, we are quickly helpless. That is all."

"But," said David, "if that were the case, wouldn't the responsible group communicate with the government, if only to give an ultimatum?"

"It would seem so, but they may be waiting their time; waiting for ripeness. Or they may be dealing with the farmers of Mars directly. The colonists have minds of their own, mistrust Earth, and, in fact, if they see their livelihood threatened, may throw in with these criminals

28

altogether. Maybe even," he puffed strenuously, "they themselves are—— But I'll make no accusations."

"And my part," said David. "What is it you would have me do?"

"Let me tell him," said Conway. "David, we want you to go to Central Laboratories on the Moon. You will be part of the research team investigating the problem. At this moment they are receiving samples of every shipment of food leaving Mars. We are bound to come across some poisoned item. Half of all items are fed to rats; the remaining portions of any fatal pieces are analyzed by all the means at our disposal."

"I see. And if Uncle Gus is right, I suppose you have another team on Mars?"

"Very experienced men. But meanwhile, will you be ready to leave for the Moon tomorrow night?"

"Certainly. But if that's the case, may I leave now to get ready?"

"Of course."

"And would there be any objection to my using my own ship?"

"Not at all."

The two scientists, alone in the room, stared down at the fairy-tale lights of the city for a long time before either spoke.

Finally Conway said, "How like Lawrence he is! But he's still so young. It will be dangerous."

Henree said, "You really think it will work?"

"Certainly!" Conway laughed. "You heard his last

question about Mars. He has no intention of going to the Moon. I know him that well. And it's the best way to protect him. The official records will say he is going to the Moon; the men at Central Laboratories are instructed to report his arrival. When he does reach Mars, there will be no reason for your conspirators, if they exist, to take him for a member of the Council, and of course he will maintain an incognito because he will be busy fooling us, he thinks."

Conway added, "He's brilliant. He may be able to do something the rest of us could not do. Fortunately, he's still young and can be maneuvered. In a few years that will be impossible. He would see through us."

Conway's communicator tinkled gently. He flipped it open. "What is it?"

"Personal communication for you, sir."

"For me? Transmit it." He looked wildly at Henree. "It can't be from the conspirators you babble about."

"Open it and see," suggested Henree.

Conway sliced the envelope open. For a moment he stared. Then he laughed a bit wildly, tossed the open sheet to Henree, and slumped back in his chair.

Henree picked it up. There were only two scrawled lines which read, "Have it your way! Mars it is." It was signed, "David."

Henree roared with laughter. "You maneuvered him all right."

And Conway could not help but join.

★ ★ ★ ★ Chapter 3

MEN FOR THE FARMS OF MARS

To a native Earthman, Earth meant Earth. It was just the third planet from that sun which was known to the inhabitants of the Galaxy as Sol. In official geography, however, Earth was more: it included all the bodies of the Solar System. Mars was as much Earth as Earth itself was, and the men and women who lived on Mars were as much Earthmen as though they lived on the home planet. Legally, at any rate. They voted for representatives in the All-Earth Congress and for Planetary President.

But that was as far as it went. The Earthmen of Mars considered themselves quite a separate and better breed, and the newcomer had a long way to go to be accepted by the Martian farmboy as anything more than a casual tourist of not much account.

David Starr found that out almost at once when he

entered the Farm Employment Building. A little man was at his heels as he walked in. A really little man. He was about five feet two and his nose would have rubbed against David's breastbone if they had stood face to face. He had pale red hair brushed straight back, a wide mouth, and the typical open-collar, double-breasted overall and hip-high, brightly colored boots of the Martian farmboy.

As David headed for the window over which glowed the legend, "Farm Employment," footsteps rattled about him, and a tenor voice cried out, "Hold on. Decelerate your footsteps, fella."

The little man was facing him.

David said, "Is there anything I can do for you?"

The little man carefully inspected him, section by section, then put out one arm and leaned negligently against the Earthman's waistline. "When did you descend the old gangplank?"

"What gangplank?"

"Pretty voluminous for an Earthie at that. Did you get cramped out there?"

"I'm from Earth, yes."

The little man brought his hands down one after the other so that they slapped sharply against his boots. It was the farmboy gesture of self-assertion.

"In that case," he said, "suppose you assume a waiting position and let a native attend to his business."

David said, "As you please."

"And if you have any objection to taking your turn, you can take it up with me when we're through or any time thereafter at your convenience. My name is Bigman. I'm John Bigman Jones, but you can ask for me anywhere in town by the name of Bigman." He paused, then added, "That, Earthie, is my cognomen. Any complaints about it?"

And David said gravely, "None at all."

Bigman said, "Right!" and left for the desk, while David, breaking into a smile as soon as the other's back was safely turned, sat down to wait.

He had been on Mars for less than twelve hours, just long enough to register his ship under an assumed name in the large sub-surface garages outside the city, take a room for the night at one of the hotels, and spend a few hours of the morning walking through the domed city.

There were only three of these cities on Mars, and their fewness was to be expected in view of the expense required to maintain the tremendous domes and to supply the torrents of power necessary to provide the temperature and gravity of Earth. This, Wingrad City, named after Robert Clark Wingrad, the first man to reach Mars, was the largest.

It was not very different from a city on Earth; it was almost a piece of Earth cut out and put on a different planet; it was as though the men on Mars, thirty-five million miles away at the very nearest, had to hide that fact from themselves somehow. In the center of town, where the ellipsoidal dome was a quarter of a mile high, there were even twenty-story buildings.

There was only one thing missing. There was no sun and no blue sky. The dome itself was translucent, and

33

when the sun shone on it, light was uniformly spread over all its ten square miles. The light intensity at any region of the dome was small so that the "sky" to a man in the city was a pale, pale yellow. The total effect, however, was about equivalent to that of a cloudy day on Earth.

When night came, the dome faded and disappeared into starless black. But then the street lights went on, and Wingrad City seemed more than ever like Earth. Within the buildings artificial light was used day and night.

David Starr looked up at the sudden sound of loud voices.

Bigman was still at the desk, shouting, "I tell you this is a case of blacklist. You've got me blacklisted, by Jupiter."

The man behind the desk seemed flustered. He had fluffy sideburns with which his fingers kept playing. He said, "We have no blacklists, Mr. Jones——"

"My name is Bigman. What's the matter? Are you afraid to exhibit friendship? You called me Bigman the first few days."

"We have no blacklists, Bigman. Farmhands just aren't in demand."

"What are you talking about? Tim Jenkins got placed day before yesterday in two minutes."

"Jenkins had experience as a rocket man."

"I can handle a rocket as well as Tim any day."

"Well, you're down here as a seeder."

"And I'm a good one. Don't they need seeders?"

"Look, Bigman," said the man behind the desk, "I have your name on the roster. That's all I can do. I'll let you know if anything turns up." He turned a concentrated attention on the record book before him, following up entries with elaborate unconcern.

Bigman turned, then shouted over his shoulder, "All right, but I'm sitting right here, and the next labor requisition you get, I'm being sent out. If they don't want me, I want to hear them say so to me. To me, do you understand? To me, J. Bigman J., personally."

The man behind the desk said nothing. Bigman took a seat, muttering. David Starr rose and approached the desk. No other farmboy had entered to dispute his place in line.

He said, "I'd like a job."

The man looked up, pulled an employment blank and hand printer toward himself. "What kind?"

"Any kind of farm work available."

The man put down his hand printer. "Are you Mars-bred?"

"No, sir. I'm from Earth."

"Sorry. Nothing open."

David said, "Well, look here. I can work, and I need work. Great Galaxy, is there a law against Earthmen working?"

"No, but there isn't much you can do on a farm without experience."

"I still need a job."

"There are lots of jobs *in* town. Next window over."

"I can't use a job in town."

35

The man behind the desk looked speculatively at David, and David had no trouble in reading the glance. Men traveled to Mars for many reasons, and one of them was that Earth had become too uncomfortable. When a search call went out for a fugitive, the cities of Mars were combed thoroughly (after all, they were part of Earth), but no one ever found a hunted man on the Mars farms. To the Farming Syndicates, the best farmboy was one who had no other place he dared go. They protected such and took care not to lose them to the Earth authorities they half-resented and more than half-despised.

"Name?" said the clerk, eyes back on the form.

"Dick Williams," said David, giving the name under which he had garaged his ship.

The clerk did not ask for identification. "Where can I get in touch with you?"

"Landis Hotel, Room 212."

"Any low-gravity experience at all?"

The questioning went on and on; most of the blanks had to be left empty. The clerk sighed, put the blank into the slot which automatically microfilmed it, filed it, and thus added it to the permanent records of the office.

He said, "I'll let you know." But he didn't sound hopeful.

David turned away. He had not expected much to come of this, but at least he had established himself as a somewhat legitimate seeker after a farming job. The next step——

He whirled. Three men were entering the employment office and the little fellow, Bigman, had hopped angrily out of his seat. He was facing them now, arms carried loosely away from his hips although he had no weapons that David could see.

The three who entered stopped, and then one of the two who brought up the rear laughed and said, "Looks as if we have Bigman, the mighty midget, here. Maybe he's looking for a job, boss." The speaker was broad across the shoulders and his nose was flattened against his face. He had a chewed-to-death, unlit cigar of green Martian tobacco in his mouth and he needed a shave badly.

"Quiet, Griswold," said the man in front. He was pudgy, not too tall, and the soft skin on his cheeks and on the back of his neck was sleek and smooth. His overall was typical Mars, of course, but it was of much finer material than that of any of the other farmboys in the room. His hip-high boots were spiraled in pink and rose.

In all his later travels on Mars, David Starr never saw two pairs of boots of identical design, never saw boots that were other than garish. It was *the* mark of individuality among the farmboys.

Bigman was approaching the three, his little chest swelling and his face twisted with anger. He said, "I want my papers out of you, Hennes. I've got a right to them."

The pudgy man in front was Hennes. He said quietly, "You're not worth any papers, Bigman."

"I can't get another job without decent papers. I worked for you for two years and did my part."

"You did a blasted lot more than your part. Out of my way." He tramped past Bigman, approached the desk, and said, "I need an experienced seeder—a good one. I want one tall enough to see in order to replace a little boy I had to get rid of."

Bigman felt that. "By Space," he yelled, "you're right I did more than my part. I was on duty when I wasn't supposed to be, you mean. I was on duty long enough to see you go driving wheels-over-sand into the desert at midnight. Only the next morning you knew nothing about it, except that I got heaved for referring to it, and without reference papers——"

Hennes looked over his shoulder, annoyed. "Griswold," he said, "throw that fool out."

Bigman did not retreat, although Griswold would have made two of him. He said in his high voice, "All right. One at a time."

But David Starr moved now, his smooth stride deceptively slow.

Griswold said, "You're in my way, friend. I've got some trash to throw out."

From behind David, Bigman cried out, "It's all right, Earthie. Let him at me."

David ignored that. He said to Griswold, "This seems to be a public place, friend. We've all got the right to be here."

Griswold said, "Let's not argue, friend." He put a hand roughly on David's shoulder as though to thrust him to one side.

But David's left hand shot up to catch the wrist of

Griswold's outstretched arm, and his right hand straight-armed the other's shoulder. Griswold went whirling backward, slamming hard against the plastic partition that divided the room in two.

"I'd *rather* argue, friend," said David.

The clerk had come to his feet with a yell. Other desk workers swarmed to the openings in the partition, but made no move to interfere. Bigman was laughing and clapping David on the back. "Pretty good for a fellow from Earth."

For the moment Hennes seemed frozen. The remaining farmboy, short and bearded, with the pasty face of one who had spent too much time under the small sun of Mars and not enough under the artificial sun lamps of the city, had allowed his mouth to drop ridiculously open.

Griswold recovered his breath slowly. He shook his head. His cigar, which had dropped to the ground, he kicked aside. Then he looked up, his eyes popping with fury. He pushed himself away from the wall and there was a momentary glint of steel that was swallowed up in his hand.

But David stepped to one side and brought up his arm. The small, crooked cylinder that ordinarily rested snugly between his upper arm and body shot down the length of his sleeve and into his gripping palm.

Hennes cried out, "Watch your step, Griswold. He's got a blaster."

"Drop your blade," said David.

Griswold swore wildly, but metal clattered against

the floor. Bigman darted forward and picked up the blade, chortling at the stubbled one's discomfiture.

David held out his hand for it and spared it a quick glance. "Nice, innocent baby for a farmboy to have," he said. "What's the law in Mars against carrying a force-blade?"

He knew it as the most vicious weapon in the Galaxy. Outwardly, it was merely a short shaft of stainless steel that was a little thicker than the haft of a knife but which could still be held nicely in the palm. Within it was a tiny motor that could generate an invisible nine-inch-long, razor-thin force-field that could cut through anything composed of ordinary matter. Armor was of no use against it, and since it could slice through bone as easily as through flesh, its stab was almost invariably fatal.

Hennes stepped between them. He said, "Where's your license for a blaster, Earthie? Put it away and we'll call it quits. Get back there, Griswold."

"Hold on," said David, as Hennes turned away. "You're looking for a man, aren't you?"

Hennes turned back, his eyebrows lifting in amusement. "I'm looking for a man. Yes."

"All right. I'm looking for a job."

"I'm looking for an experienced seeder. Do you qualify?"

"Well, no."

"Have you ever harvested? Can you handle a sand-car? In short, you're just, if I may judge from your costume"—and he stepped back as though to get a better over-all view—"an Earthman who happens to be handy with a blaster. I can't use you."

"Not even," David's voice fell to a whisper, "if I tell you that I'm interested in food poisoning?"

Hennes's face didn't change; his eyes didn't flicker. He said, "I don't see your point."

"Think harder, then." He was smiling thinly, and there was little humor in that smile.

Hennes said, "Working on a Mars farm isn't easy."

"I'm not the easy type," said David.

The other looked over his rangy frame again. "Well, maybe you're not. All right, we'll lodge and feed you, start you with three changes of clothing and a pair of boots. Fifty dollars the first year, payable at the end of the year. If you don't work out the year, the fifty is forfeited."

"Fair enough. What type of work?"

"The only kind you can do. General helper at the chowhouse. If you learn, you'll move up; if not, that's where you spend the year."

"Done. What about Bigman?"

Bigman, who had been staring from one to the other, squawked, "No, sir. I don't work for that sand-bug, and I wouldn't advise you to, either."

David said over his shoulder, "How about a short stretch in return for papers of reference?"

"Well," said Bigman, "a month, maybe."

Hennes said, "Is he a friend of yours?"

David nodded. "I won't come without him."

"I'll take him, too, then. One month, and he's to keep

his mouth shut. No pay, except his papers. Let's get out of here. My sand-car's outside."

The five left, David and Bigman bringing up the rear.

Bigman said, "I owe you a favor, friend. You may collect at will."

The sand-car was open just then, but David could see the slots into which panels could slide in order that it might be enclosed against the drifting dust storms of Mars. The wheels were broad to minimize the tendency to sink when crossing the soft drifts. The area of glass was reduced to a minimum and, where it existed, merged into the surrounding metal as though they had been welded together.

The streets were moderately crowded, but no one paid any attention to the very common sight of sand-cars and farmboys.

Hennes said, "We'll sit in front. You and your friend may sit in back, Earthman."

He had moved into the driver's seat as he spoke. The controls were in the middle of the front partition, with the windshield centered above. Griswold took the seat at Hennes's right.

Bigman moved into the rear and David followed him. Someone was behind him. David half turned as Bigman called suddenly, "Watch out!"

It was the second of Hennes's henchmen who was now crouching in the car door, his pasty bearded face snarling and taut. David moved quickly, but it was far too late.

His last sight was that of the gleaming muzzle of a

weapon in the henchman's hand, and then he was conscious of a soft purring noise. There was scarcely any sensation to it, and a distant, distant voice said, "All right, Zukis. Get in back and keep watch," in words that seemed to come from the end of a long tunnel. There was a last momentary feeling of motion forward, and then there was complete nothingness.

David Starr slumped forward in his seat, and the last signs of life about him vanished.

★ ★ ★ ★ Chapter 4

ALIEN LIFE

Ragged patches of light floated past David Starr. Slowly he became aware of a tremendous tingling all about him and a separate pressure on his back. The back pressure resolved itself into the fact that he was lying face up on a hard mattress. The tingling he knew to be the aftermath of a stun-gun, a weapon whose radiation worked upon the nerve centers at the base of the brain.

Before light became coherent, before he was thoroughly aware of his surroundings, he felt his shoulders being shaken and the distant sting of sharp slaps on his cheeks. The light washed into his open eyes and he brought his tingling arm up to ward off the next slap.

It was Bigman leaning over him, his little rabbity face with its round snub nose nearly touching his. He said, "By Ganymede, I thought they finished you for good."

David brought himself up to an aching elbow. He said, "It almost feels as if they did. Where are we?"

"In the farm lockup. It's no use trying to get out, either. The door's locked; the windows are barred." He looked depressed.

David felt under his arms. They had removed his blasters. Naturally! So much was to be expected. He said, "Did they stun you, too, Bigman?"

Bigman shook his head. "Zukis horizontaled me with the gun butt." He fingered a region of his skull with gingerly distaste. Then he swelled, "But I nearly broke his arm first."

There was the sound of footsteps outside the door. David sat up and waited. Hennes entered, and with him there came an older man, with a long, tired-looking face set off by faded blue eyes under bushy gray eyebrows that seemed fixed in a permanent furrow. He was dressed in city costume, which was much like that of Earth. He even lacked the Martian hip boots.

Hennes spoke to Bigman first. "Get out to the chow-house and the first time you sneeze without permission you'll be broken in two."

Bigman scowled, waved to David with an "I'll be seeing you, Earthman," and swaggered out with a clattering of boots.

Hennes watched him leave and locked the door behind him. He turned to the man with the gray eyebrows. "This is the one, Mr. Makian. He calls himself Williams."

"You took a chance stunning him, Hennes. If you had

killed him, a valuable lead might have gone with the canal-dust."

Hennes shrugged. "He was armed. We could take no chances. In any case, he's here, sir."

They were discussing him, David thought, as though he weren't there or were just another inanimate part of the bed.

Makian turned to him, his eyes hard. "You, there, I own this ranch. Over a hundred miles in any direction is all Makian. I say who is to be free and who is to be in prison; who works and who starves; even who lives and who dies. Do you understand me?"

"Yes," said David.

"Then answer frankly, and you'll have nothing to fear. Try to hide anything and we'll have it out of you one way or another. We may have to kill you. Do you still understand me?"

"Perfectly."

"Is your name Williams?"

"It's the only name I will give on Mars."

"Fair enough. What do you know about food poisoning?"

David swung his feet off the bed. He said, "Look, my sister died over an afternoon snack of bread and jam. She was twelve years old, and lay there dead with the jam still on her face. We called the doctor. He said it was food poisoning and told us not to eat anything in the house till he came back with certain analytical equipment. He never came back.

"Somebody else came instead. Someone with a great

deal of authority. He had plain-clothes men to escort him. He had us describe all that had happened. He said to us, 'It was a heart attack.' We told him that was ridiculous because my sister had nothing wrong with her heart, but he wouldn't listen to us. He told us that if we spread ridiculous stories about food poisoning, we would get in trouble. Then he took the jar of jam with him. He was even angry with us for having wiped the jam from my sister's lips.

"I tried to get in touch with our doctor, but his nurse would never admit he was in. I broke into his office and found him there, but all he would say was that he had made a mistaken diagnosis. He seemed afraid to talk about it. I went to the police, but they wouldn't listen.

"The jar of jam the men took away was the only thing in the house my sister ate that day that the rest of the family hadn't eaten as well. That jar was freshly opened and it was imported from Mars. We're old-fashioned people and like the old food. That was the only Mars product in the house. I tried to find out through the newspapers whether there had been any other cases of food poisoning. It all seemed so suspicious to me. I even went to International City. I quit my job and decided that in one way or another I would find out what had killed my sister and try to nail anyone that might be responsible. Everywhere I hit a blank, and then there came policemen with a warrant for my arrest.

"I was almost expecting that, and got out a step ahead of them. I came to Mars for two reasons. First, it was the only way to keep out of jail (though it doesn't seem so now, does it?), and second, because of one thing I *did* find out. There were two or three suspicious deaths in the restaurants of International City and in each case they were at restaurants which featured Martian cuisines. So I decided the answer was on Mars."

Makian was running a thick thumb down the long line of his chin. He said, "The yarn hangs together, Hennes. What do you think?"

"I say, get names and dates, and check the story. We don't know who this man is."

Makian sounded almost querulous. "You know we can't do that, Hennes. I don't want to do anything that would spread news of all this mess. It would break the entire Syndicate." He turned to David. "I'm going to send Benson to speak to you; he's our agronomist." Then, again to Hennes, "You stay here till Benson comes."

It was about half an hour before Benson came. During that interval David leaned carelessly back on the cot paying no attention to Hennes, who, for his part, played the same sort of game.

Then the door opened and a voice said, "I'm Benson." It was a gentle, hesitant voice and it belonged to a round-faced individual of about forty, with thinning sandy hair and rimless eyeglasses. His small mouth spread itself in a smile.

Benson went on, "And you, I suppose, are Williams?"

"That's right," said David Starr.

Benson looked carefully at the young Earthman, as

though he were analyzing him by eye. He said, "Are you disposed to violence?"

"I'm unarmed," David pointed out, "and surrounded by a farm full of men quite ready to kill me if I step out of line."

"Quite right. Would you leave us, Hennes?"

Hennes jumped to his feet in protest. "That's not safe, Benson."

"Please, Hennes." Benson's mild eyes peered over his spectacles.

Hennes growled, clapped one hand against a boot in disgruntlement, and walked out the door. Benson locked it behind him.

"You see, Williams," he said apologetically, "in the last half-year I've grown to be an important man here. Even Hennes listens to me. I'm still not used to it." He smiled again. "Tell me. Mr. Makian says you actually witnessed a death by this strange food poisoning."

"My sister's."

"Oh!" Benson flushed. "I'm dreadfully sorry. I know it must be a painful subject to you, but might I have the details? It's very important."

David repeated the story he had earlier told Makian.

Benson said, "And it happened as quickly as that."

"It could only have been five to ten minutes after she had eaten."

"Terrible. Terrible. You have no idea how distressing all this is." He was rubbing his hands together nervously. "In any case, Williams, I'd like to fill in the story for you. You've guessed most of it, anyway, and, somehow,

49

I feel responsible to you for what happened to your sister. All of us here on Mars are responsible until such time as we clear up the mystery. You see, this has been going on for months now, these poisonings. Not many, but enough to have us at our wit's end.

"We've traced back the poisoned foodstuffs and we are certain they come from no one farm. But one thing did turn up: all the poisoned food is shipped out of Wingrad City; the other two cities on Mars are clean so far. That would seem to indicate that the source of infection is within the city, and Hennes has been working on the assumption. He has taken to riding to the city, nights, on detective expeditions of his own, but he has turned up nothing."

"I see. That explains Bigman's remarks," said David.

"Eh?" Benson's face twisted in puzzlement, then cleared. "Oh, you mean the little fellow who goes about shouting all the time. Yes, he caught Hennes leaving once, and Hennes had him thrown out. Hennes is a most impulsive man. In any case, I think Hennes is wrong. Naturally all the poison would travel through Wingrad City. It is the shipping point for the entire hemisphere.

"Now Mr. Makian himself believes the infection to be deliberately spread through human agency. At least he and several others of the Syndicate have received messages offering to buy their farms for a ridiculously small sum. There is no mention of the poisoning and no evidence whatsoever of any connection between the offers to buy and this horrible business."

David was listening intently. He said, "And who makes these offers to buy?"

"Why, how should we know? I have seen the letters and they only say that if the offers are accepted, the Syndicate is to broadcast a coded message over a particular sub-etheric waveband. The price offer, the letters say, will decrease by 10 per cent each month."

"And the letters can't be traced?"

"I'm afraid not. They pass through the ordinary mails with an 'Asteroid' postmark. How can one search the Asteroids?"

"Have the Planetary Police been informed?"

Benson laughed softly. "Do you think Mr. Makian, or any of the Syndicate for that matter, would call in the police for a thing like this? This is a declaration of personal war to them. You don't properly appreciate the Martian mentality, Mr. Williams. You don't run to the law when you're in trouble unless you're willing to confess it's something you can't handle yourself. No farmboy is ever willing to do that. I've suggested that the information be submitted to the Council of Science, but Mr. Makian wouldn't even do that. He said the Council was working on the poisoning without success, and if that were the kind of darned fools they were, he would do without them. And that's where I come in."

"You're working on the poisoning too?"

"That's right. I'm the agronomist here."

"That's the title Mr. Makian gave you."

"Uh-huh. Strictly speaking, an agronomist is a person who specializes in scientific agriculture. I've been trained in principles of fertility maintenance, crop rotation, and matters of that sort. I've always specialized in Martian problems. There aren't many of us and so one can get a rather good position, even though the farmboys some-times lose patience with us and think we're just college idiots without practical experience. Anyway, I've had additional training as well in botany and bacteriology, so I've been put in charge by Mr. Makian of the entire re-search program on Mars with respect to the poisoning. The other members of the Syndicate are co-operating."

"And what have you found out, Mr. Benson?"

"Actually as little as the Council of Science, which is not surprising considering how little I have in the way of equipment and help in comparison with them. But I have developed certain theories. The poisoning is too rapid for anything but a bacterial toxin. At least if we consider the nerve degeneration that takes place and the other symptoms. I suspect Martian bacteria."

"What!"

"There *is* Martian life, you know. When Earthmen first arrived, Mars was covered with simple forms of life. There were giant algae whose blue-green color was seen telescopically even before space-travel was invented. There were bacteria-like forms that lived on the algae and even little insect-like creatures that were free-mov-ing, yet manufactured their own food like plants."

"Do they still exist?"

"Why, certainly. We clear them off the land com-pletely before converting areas to our own farms and introduce our own strains of bacteria, the ones that are necessary to plant growth. Out in the uncultivated areas, however, Martian life still flourishes."

"But how can they be affecting our plants, then."

"That's a good question. You see, Martian farms are not like the Earth farm lands you're used to. On Mars, the farms are not open to sun and air. The sun on Mars doesn't give enough heat for Earth plants and there is no rain. But there is good, fertile soil and there is quite enough carbon dioxide which the plants live on primarily. So crops on Mars are grown under vast sheets of glass. They are seeded, cared for, and harvested by nearly automatic machinery so that our farmboys are machinists more than anything else. The farms are artificially watered by a system of planet-wide piping that carries back to the polar icecaps.

"I tell you this so you will realize that it would be difficult to infect plants ordinarily. The fields are closed and guarded from all directions except from beneath."

"What does that mean?" asked David.

"It means that underneath are the famous Martian caverns and within them there may be intelligent Martians."

"You mean Martian *men?*"

"Not men. But organisms as intelligent as man. I have reason to believe that there *are* Martian intelligences that are probably anxious to drive us intruding Earthmen from the face of their planet!"

★ ★ ★ ★ Chapter 5

DINNERTIME

"What reason?" demanded David.

Benson looked embarrassed. He moved one hand slowly over his head, smoothing the sparse strands of light hair that did not manage to hide the pink streaks of hairless skull that lay between. He said, "None that I could convince the Council of Science with. None that I could even present to Mr. Makian. But I believe I'm right."

"Is it anything you would care to talk about?"

"Well, I don't know. Frankly, it's been a long time since I've spoken to anyone but farmboys. You're a college man obviously. What did you major in?"

"History," said David promptly. "My thesis concerned the international politics of the early atomic age."

"Oh." Benson looked disappointed. "Any courses in science at all?"

"I had a couple in chemistry; one in zoology."

"I see. It occurred to me that I might be able to convince Mr. Makian to let you help me in my laboratory. It wouldn't be much of a job, especially since you have no scientific training, but it would be better than what Hennes will have you doing."

"Thank you, Mr. Benson. But about the Martians?"

"Oh yes. It's simple enough. You may not know it but there are extensive caves under the Martian surface, perhaps several miles under. So much is known from earthquake data, or, rather, Marsquake data. Some investigators claim they are merely the result of natural water action in the days when Mars still had oceans, but then radiation has been picked up that has its source beneath the soil and which can't have a human source but must have some intelligent source. The signals are too orderly to be anything else.

"It makes sense, really, if you stop to think about it. In the youth of the planet there was sufficient water and oxygen to support life, but with a gravity only two fifths that of Earth, both substances leaked slowly away into space. If there were intelligent Martians, they must have been able to foresee that. They might have built huge caverns well underneath their soil, into which they could retire with enough water and air to continue indefinitely, if they kept their population stable. Now suppose these Martians found that their planet's surface was harboring intelligent life once more—life from another planet. Suppose they resented it or feared our eventual interference with them. What we call food poisoning might be bacteriological warfare."

David said thoughtfully, "Yes, I see your point."

"But would the Syndicate? Or the Council of Science? Well, never mind. I'll have you working for me soon, and perhaps we'll be able to convince them yet."

He smiled and held out a soft hand which was swallowed up in David Starr's large one.

"I think they'll be letting you out now," Benson said.

They did let him out, and for the first time David had the chance to observe the heart of a Martian farm. It was domed, of course, as the city had been. David had been sure of that from the instant he had regained consciousness. You couldn't expect to be breathing free air and living under Earth-strength gravity unless you were within a powered dome.

Naturally the dome was much smaller than that of a city. At its highest it was only about one hundred feet, its translucent structure visible in all its details, strings of white fluorescent lights outdoing the translucent glimmer of the sunlight. The whole structure covered about half a square mile.

After the first evening, however, David had little time to extend his observations. The farm dome seemed full of men and they all had to be fed three times a day. In the evenings particularly, with the day's work done, there seemed no end to them. Stolidly he would stand behind the chow table while farmboys with plastic platters moved past him. The platters, David found out eventually, were manufactured especially for Martian

56

farm use. Under the heat of human hands they could be molded and closed about the food at such times as it was necessary to carry meals out to the desert. Molded so, they kept the sand out and the heat in. Within the farm dome they could be flattened out again and used in the usual way.

The farmboys paid David little attention. Only Bigman, whose lithe frame slipped among the tables replacing sauce bottles and spice containers, waved to him. It was a terrible drop in social position for the little fellow, but he was philosophical about it.

"It's only for a month," he had explained one time in the kitchen, when they were preparing the day's stew and the head cook had left on his own business for a few minutes, "and most of the fellows know the score and are making it easy for me. Of course there's Griswold, Zukis, and that bunch: the rats that try to get somewhere by licking Hennes' boots. But what in Space do I care? It's only a few weeks."

Another time he said, "Don't let it bother you about the boys not cottoning to you. They know you're an Earthman, see, and they don't know you're pretty good for an Earthman, like I do. Hennes is always poking about after me, or else Griswold is, to make sure I don't talk to them, or else they would have heard the facts from me. But they'll get wise."

But the process was taking time. For David, it remained the same: a farmboy and his platter; a dollop of mashed potatoes, a ladle of peas, and a small steak (animal food was much scarcer on Mars than plant food, since meat had to be imported from Earth). The farm-boy then helped himself to a sliver of cake and a cup of coffee. Then another farmboy with another platter; another dollop of mashed potatoes, another ladle of peas, and so on. To them, it seemed, David Starr was just an Earthman with a ladle in one hand and a large-tined fork in the other. He wasn't even a face; just a ladle and a fork.

The cook stuck his head through the door, his little eyes peering piggily over the sagging pouches beneath. "Hey, Williams. Rattle your legs and get some food into the special mess."

Makian, Benson, Hennes, and any others who were considered especially worthy in point of view of position or of length of service dined in a room by themselves. They sat at tables and had the food brought to them. David had been through this before. He prepared special platters and brought them into the room on a wheeled service table.

He threaded his way quietly through the tables, beginning with the one at which Makian, Hennes, and two others sat. At Benson's table he lingered. Benson accepted his platter with a smile and a "How are you?" and proceeded to eat with relish. David, with an air of conscientiousness, brushed at invisible crumbs. His mouth managed to get itself close to Benson's ears and his lips scarcely moved as he said, "Anyone ever get poisoned here at the farm?"

Benson started at the sudden sound of words and looked quickly at David. As quickly he looked away, tried to appear indifferent. He shook his head in a sharp negative.

"The vegetables are Martian, aren't they?" murmured David.

A new voice sounded in the room. It was a rough yell from the other end of the room.

"By Space, you long Earth jackass, get a move on!"

It was Griswold, his face still stubbled. He must shave sometimes, David thought, since the stubble never grew longer, but no one ever seemed to see it shorter, either.

Griswold was at the last table to be visited. He was still mumbling, his anger boiling over.

His lips drew back. "Bring over that platter, dish-jockey. Faster. Faster."

David did so, but without hurry, and Griswold's hand, with the fork in it, jabbed quickly. David moved more quickly, and the fork clanged sharply against the hard plastic of the tray.

Balancing the tray in one hand, David caught Griswold's fist with the other. His grip grew tight. The other three at the table pushed back their chairs and rose.

David's voice, low, icy, and dead level, sounded just high enough to be heard by Griswold. "Drop it and ask for your ration decently, or you'll have it all at once."

Griswold writhed, but David maintained his hold. David's knee in the back of Griswold's chair prevented the farmboy from pushing away from the table.

"Ask nicely," said David. He smiled, deceptively gentle. "Like a man with breeding."

Griswold was panting harshly. The fork dropped

from between his numbed fingers. He growled, "Let me have the tray."

"Is that all?"

"Please." He spat it out.

David lowered the tray and released the other's fist from which the blood had been crushed, leaving it white. Griswold massaged it with his other hand and reached for his fork. He looked about him, mad with fury, but there was only amusement or indifference in the eyes that met his. The farms on Mars were hard; each man had to care for himself.

Makian was standing. "Williams," he called.

David approached. "Sir?"

Makian made no direct reference to what had just occurred, but he stood there for a moment, looking carefully at David, as though he were seeing him for the first time and liked what he saw. He said, "Would you like to join the checkup tomorrow?"

"The checkup, sir? What is that?" Unobtrusively he surveyed the table. Makian's steak was gone, but his peas remained behind and the mashed potatoes were scarcely touched. He had not the grit, apparently, of Hennes, who had left a clean platter.

"The checkup is the monthly drive through all the farm to check on the plant rows. It's an old farm custom. We check on possible accidental breaks in the glass, on the condition and workings of the irrigation pipes and farm machinery, also on possible poaching. We need as many good men as possible out on the checkup."

"I'd like to go, sir."

"Good! I think you'll do." Makian turned to Hennes, who had been listening throughout with cold and unemotional eyes. "I like the boy's style, Hennes. We may be able to make a farmboy out of him. And, Hennes——" His voice sank and David, moving away, could no longer catch it, but from the quick hooded glance Makian cast in the direction of Griswold's table, it could not have been very complimentary to the veteran farmboy.

David Starr caught the footstep inside his own partitioning and acted even before he was fully awake. He slipped off the far side of the bed and underneath. He caught the glimpse of bare feet glimmering whitely in the pale light of the residual fluorescents shining through the window. The residuals were allowed to burn in the farm dome during the sleeping period to avoid darkness too inconveniently black.

David waited, heard the rustle of the sheets as hands probed uselessly through the bed, then a whisper. "Earthman! Earthman! Where in Space——"

David touched one of the feet and was rewarded by a sudden withdrawal and a sharp intake of breath.

There was a pause and then a head, shapeless in the dusk, was near his. "Earthman? You there?"

"Where else would I be sleeping, Bigman? I like it here under the bed."

The little fellow fumed and whispered peevishly, "You might have squeezed a yell out of me and then I would have been in the stew to my ears. I've got to talk to you."

61

"Now's your chance." David chuckled softly and crawled back into bed.

Bigman said, "You're a suspicious space bug for an Earthman."

"You bet," said David. "I intend living a long life."

"If you're not careful, you won't."

"No?"

"No. I'm foolish to be here. If I'm caught, I'll never get my reference papers. It's just that you helped me when I could use it, and it's my turn to pay back. What was it you did to this louse, Griswold?"

"Just a little mixup in the special mess."

"A little mixup? He was raving mad. It was all Hennes could do to hold him back."

"Is this what you came to tell me, Bigman?"

"Part of it. They were behind the garage just after lights-out. They didn't know I was around, and I didn't tell them. Anyway, Hennes was yanking the stuffings out of Griswold; first for starting something with you when the Old Man was watching; and second, for not having the sand to finish once he had started it. Griswold was too mad to talk sense. Near as I could judge, he was just gargling something about how he would have your gizzard. Hennes said——" He broke off. "Listen, didn't you tell me that Hennes was all clear as far as you were concerned?"

"He seems so."

"Those midnight trips——"

"You only saw him once."

"Once is enough. If it was legitimate, why can't you give me the straight stuff?"

"It's not mine to give, Bigman, but it all seems legitimate."

"If that's the case, what's he got against you? Why doesn't he call off his dogs?"

"What do you mean?"

"Well, when Griswold finished talking, Hennes said he was to hold off. He said you would be out on checkup tomorrow and that would be the time. So I thought I'd come and warn you, Earthman. Better stay off checkup."

David's voice remained unflurried. "Checkup would be time for what? Did Hennes say?"

"I didn't hear past that. They moved away and I couldn't follow, or I would have been out in the open. But I assume it's pretty plain."

"Maybe. But suppose we try to find out for sure exactly what they're after."

Bigman leaned close, as though he were trying to extract a reading from David's face despite the gloom. "How do you mean?"

David said, "How do you suppose. I'll be at the checkup and give the boys a chance to show me."

"You can't do that," gasped Bigman. "You couldn't handle yourself on a checkup against them. You don't know anything about Mars, you poor Earthman you."

"Then," said David phlegmatically, "it could mean suicide, I suppose. Let's wait and see." He patted Bigman on the shoulder, turned over, and went to sleep again.

★ ★ ★ ★ Chapter 6

"SAND AWAY!"

Checkup excitement began within the farm dome as soon as the main fluorescents were turned on. There was a wild noise and a mad scurry. Sand-cars were brought out in rows, each farmboy tending his own.

Makian was here and there, never too long at any one point. Hennes, in his flat, efficient voice, assigned the parties and set the routes across the farm's vast expanse. He looked up as he passed David and stopped.

"Williams," he said, "are you still of a mind to be on the checkup?"

"I wouldn't miss it."

"All right then. Since you haven't any car of your own, I'll assign you one out of general stock. Once it's assigned, it's yours to take care of and keep in working condition. Any repairs or damage which we consider avoidable will come out of your pay. Understood?"

"Fair enough."

"I'll put you on Griswold's team. I know that you and he don't get along, but he's our best man in the fields and you're an Earthie without experience. I wouldn't care to load you onto a lesser man. Can you drive a sand-car?"

"I think I can handle any moving vehicle with a little practice."

"You can, eh? We'll give you your chance to make good on that." He was about to step away when his eyes caught something. He barked, "And where do you think you're going?"

Bigman had just stepped into the assembly room. He was in a new outfit and his boots had been polished to mirror-shine. His hair was slicked down and his face was scrubbed and pink. He drawled, "On the checkup, Hennes—*Mister* Hennes. I'm not on detention and I still have my rating as licensed farmboy even though you have put me on chow detail. That means I can go on checkup. It also means I have a right to my old car and my old squad."

Hennes shrugged. "You read the rule books a lot, and that's what they say, I suppose. But one more week, Bigman, one more week. After that, if you ever show your nose anywhere on Makian territory I'll have a real man step on you and squash you."

Bigman made a threatening gesture at Hennes's retreating back and then turned to David. "Ever used a nosepiece, Earthman?"

"Never actually. I've heard about them, of course."

"Hearing isn't using. I've checked an extra one out for you. Look, let me show you how to get it on. No, no, get your thumbs out of there. Now watch how I hold my hands. That's right. Now over the head and make sure the straps aren't twisted in the back of the neck, or you'll end with a headache. Now can you see through them?"

The upper part of David's face was transformed into a plastic-encased monstrosity, and the double hose leading from the oxygen cylinders up each side of his chin subtracted further from any appearance of humanity.

"Do you have trouble breathing?" asked Bigman.

David was struggling, fighting to suck in air. He yanked the nosepiece off. "How do you turn it on? There's no gauge."

Bigman was laughing. "That's the return for the scare you gave me last night. You don't need a gauge. The cylinders automatically feed oxygen as soon as the warmth and pressure of your face trip a contact; and it automatically closes off when you take it off."

"Then there's something wrong with it. I——"

"Nothing wrong with it. It feeds at a gas pressure of one fifth normal to match the pressure of the Mars atmosphere, and you can't suck it in out here when you're fighting the pressure of a normal Earth atmosphere. Out there in the desert it will be fine. And it will be enough, too, because even though it's one fifth normal, it's all oxygen. You'll have as much oxygen as you always had. Just remember one thing: breathe in through your nose but breathe out through your mouth.

If you breathe out through your nose, you'll fog up your eyepieces, and that won't be good."

He strutted about David's tall, straight body and shook his head. "Don't know what to do about your boots. Black and white! You look like a garbage detail or something." He glanced down at his own chartreuse-and-vermilion creations with more than a little complacency.

David said, "I'll manage. You'd better get to your car. It looks as though they're getting ready to move."

"You're right. Well, take it easy. Watch out for the gravity change. That's hard to take if you're not used to it. And, Earthman——"

"Well."

"Keep your eyes open. You know what I mean."

"Thanks. I shall."

The sand-cars were lining up now in squares of nine. There were more than a hundred all told, each with its farmboy peering over its tires and controls. Each vehicle had its handmade signs intended as humor. The sand-car trundled out for David was speckled with such signs from half-a-dozen previous owners, beginning with a "Watch Out, Girls" circling the bullet-like prow of the car and ending with a "This Ain't No Dust Storm, This Is Me," on the rear bumper.

David climbed in and closed the door. It fit tightly. Not even a seam showed. Immediately above his head there was the filtered and refiltered vent that allowed equalization of air pressure within and without the car. The glass was not quite clear. It had a faint misting that was proof of dozens of dust storms met and weathered.

David found the controls familiar enough. They were standard for ground cars, for the most part. The few unfamiliar buttons explained themselves upon manipulation.

Griswold came past, gesturing at him furiously. He opened his door.

Griswold yelled, "Get your front flaps down, you jerk. We're not heading into any storm."

David searched for the proper button and found it on the steering-wheel shaft. The windshields, which looked as though they were welded to metal, disengaged themselves and sank down into sockets. Visibility improved. Of course, he thought. Mars's atmosphere would scarcely raise wind enough to disturb them, and this was Martian summer. It would not be too cold.

A voice called, "Hey, Earthman!" He looked up. Bigman was waving at him. He was in Griswold's group of nine also. David waved back.

A section of the dome lifted up. Nine cars trundled in, moving sluggishly. The section closed behind them. Minutes passed, then it opened, empty, and nine more moved in.

Griswold's voice sounded suddenly and loudly next to David's ear. David turned and saw the small receiver in the car top just behind his head. The small grilled opening at the head of the steering-wheel shaft was a mouthpiece.

"Squad eight, ready?"

The voices sounded consecutively: "Number one, ready." "Number two, ready." "Number three, ready."

68

There was a pause after number six. Just a few seconds. David then called, "Number seven, ready." There followed "Number eight, ready." Bigman's reedy tones came last. "Number nine, ready."

The dome section was raising again and the cars ahead of David began moving. David slowly stepped on the resistor, cutting the coils, allowing electricity to pour into the motor. His sand-car leaped ahead, all but crashing into the rear of the one in front. He let out the resistor with a jerk and felt the car tremble beneath him. Gently he babied it along. The section enclosed them like a small tunnel, shutting off behind.

He became conscious of the hiss of air being pumped out of the section back into the dome proper. He felt his heart begin to pound, but his hands were steady upon the wheel.

His clothing bellied away from him and the air was seeping out along the cylindrical line where boots met thigh. There was a tingling in his hands and chin, a feeling of puffiness, of distention. He swallowed repeatedly, to relieve the gathering pain in his ears. After five minutes he found himself panting in an effort to gather enough oxygen for his needs.

The others were slipping on their nosepieces. He did the same, and this time oxygen slid smoothly up his nostrils. He breathed deeply, puffing it out through his mouth. His arms and feet still tingled, but the feeling was beginning to die away.

And now the section was opening ahead of them, and the flat, ruddy sands of Mars glittered in the sun's feeble light. There was a yell in unison from eight farmboy throats as the section lifted.

"Sand awa-a-a-ay!" and the first cars in line began to move.

It was the traditional farmboy cry, made thin and almost soprano in the thin air of Mars.

David let in the resistor and crawled across the line that marked the boundary between dome metal and Martian soil.

And it hit him!

The sudden gravity change was like a sharp fall of a thousand feet. One hundred and twenty pounds of his two hundred disappeared as he crossed the line, and it left him by way of the pit of his stomach. He clutched at the wheel as the sensation of fall, fall, *fall* persisted. The sand-car veered wildly.

There was the sound of Griswold's voice, which maintained its hoarseness even in the incongruous hollowness forced upon it by the thin air which carried sound waves so poorly. "Number seven! Back in line!"

David fought with the wheel, fought with his own sensations, fought to make himself see clearly. He dragged at the oxygen through his nosepiece and slowly the worst passed.

He could see Bigman looking anxiously in his direction. He took one hand away from the wheel momentarily to wave, then concentrated on the road.

The Martian desert was almost flat, flat and bare. Not even a scrub of vegetation existed here. This particular area had been dead and deserted for who knew how many thousands or millions of years. The thought suddenly struck him that perhaps he was wrong. Perhaps the desert sands had been coated with blue-green microorganisms until Earthmen had come and burned them away to make room for their farms.

The cars ahead trailed faint dust that rose slowly, as if it were part of a motion-picture film that had been slowed down. It settled as slowly.

David's car was trailing badly. He added speed and still more speed, and found that something was going wrong. The others, ahead of him, were hugging the ground but he, himself, was bounding like a jackrabbit. At every trifling imperfection in the ground surface, at every projecting line of rock, his car took off. It drifted lazily up into the air, inches high, its wheels whining against nothing. It came down as gently, then lurched forward with a jerk as the straining wheels caught hold.

It caused him to lose ground, and when he poured the juice in to gain again, the jumping grew worse. It was the low gravity that did it, of course, but the others managed to compensate for it. He wondered how.

It was getting cold. Even at Martian summer, he guessed the temperature to be barely above freezing. He could look directly at the sun in the sky. It was a dwarfed sun in a purple sky in which he could make out three or four stars. The air was too thin to blank them out or to scatter light in such a manner as to form the sky-blue of Earth.

Griswold's voice was sounding again: "Cars one, four,

and seven to the left. Cars two, five, and eight to the center. Cars three, six, and nine to the right. Cars two and three will be in charge of their sub-sections."

Griswold's car, number one, was beginning to curl to the left, and David, following it with his eyes, noticed the dark line on the leftward horizon. Number four was following one, and David turned his wheel sharply left to match the angle of veer.

What followed caught him by surprise. His car went into a rapid skid, scarcely allowing him time to realize it. He yanked desperately at the wheel, spinning it in the direction of skid. He shut off all power and felt the wheels rasp as the car whirled onward. The desert circled before him, so that only its redness could make any impression.

And then there was Bigman's thin cry through the receiver, "Stamp on the emergency traction. It's just to the right of the resistors."

David probed desperately for the emergency traction, whatever it was, but his aching feet found nothing. The dark line on the horizon appeared before him and then vanished. It was much sharper now, and broader. Even in that rapid flash, its nature became appallingly evident. It was one of the fissures of Mars, long and straight. Like the far more numerous ones on Earth's Moon, they were cracks in the planetary surface, made as the world dried through millions of years. They were up to a hundred feet across and no man had plumbed their depth.

"It's a pink, stubby button," yelled Bigman. "Stamp everywhere."

David did so, and there was a sudden slight yielding beneath his toes. The swift motion of his sand-car became a rebellious grinding that tore at him. The dust came up in clouds, choking him and obscuring everything.

He bent over the wheel and waited. The car was definitely slowing. And then, finally, it stopped.

He sat back and breathed quietly for a moment. Then he withdrew his nosepiece, wiped the inner surfaces while the cold air stung at nose and eyes, and replaced it. His clothes were ruddy gray with dust and his chin was caked with it. He could feel its dryness upon his lips, and the interior of his car was filthy with it.

The two other cars of his sub-section had pulled up next to him. Griswold was climbing out of one, his stubbled face made monstrously ugly by the nosepiece. David was suddenly aware of the reason for the popularity of beards and stubble among the farmboys. They were protection against the cold, thin wind of Mars.

Griswold was snarling, showing yellowed and broken teeth. He said, "Earthman, the repairs for this sand-car will come right out of your wages. You had Hennes' warning."

David opened the door and climbed out. From outside, the car was a worse wreck still, if that were possible. The tires were torn and from them projected the huge teeth which were obviously the "emergency traction."

He said, "Not one cent comes out of my wages, Griswold. There was something wrong with the car."

"That's for sure. The driver. A stupid, dumb-lug driver, that's what's wrong with the car."

Another car came squealing up, and Griswold turned to it.

His stubble seemed to bristle. "Get the blast out of here, you cinch-bug. Get on with your job."

Bigman jumped out of his car. "Not till I take a look at the Earthman's car."

Bigman weighed less than fifty pounds on Mars, and in one long, flat leap he was at David's side. He bent for a moment, then straightened. He said, "Where are the weight-rods, Griswold?"

David said, "What are the weight-rods, Bigman?"

The little fellow spoke rapidly. "When you take these sand-cars out into low gravity, you put foot-thick beams over each of the axles. You take them out when you're on high grav. I'm sorry, fella, but I never once thought that this might be what——"

David stopped him. His lips drew back. It would explain why his car had floated upward at each bump while the others were glued to the soil. He turned to Griswold. "Did you know they were gone?"

Griswold swore. "Each man is responsible for his own car. If you didn't notice they were gone, that's your negligence."

All the cars were now on the scene. A circle of hairy men were forming around the three, quiet, attentive, not interfering.

Bigman stormed. "You big hunk of silica, the man's a tenderfoot. He can't be expected to——"

"Quiet, Bigman," said David. "This is my job. I ask you again, Griswold. Did you know about this in advance?"

"And I told you, Earthie. In the desert a man has to watch himself. I'm not going to mother you."

"All right. In that case I'll watch myself right now." David looked about. They were almost at the edge of the fissure. Another ten feet and he would have been a dead man. "However, you'll have to watch yourself, too, because I'm taking your car. You can drive mine back to the farm dome or you can stay here for all I care."

"By Mars!" Griswold's hand shot to his hip and there was a sudden rough cry from the circle of watching men.

"Fair fight! Fair fight!"

The code of the Martian deserts was a hard one, but it drew the line at advantages considered unfair. That was understood and *enforced*. Only by such mutual precautions could any man be protected from an eventual force-knife in the back or blast-gun in the belly.

Griswold looked at the hard faces about him. He said, "We'll have it out back in the dome. On your jobs, men."

David said, "I'll see you in the dome if you wish. Meanwhile, step aside."

He walked forward unhurriedly, and Griswold stepped back. "You stupid greenhorn. We can't have a fist-fight with nosepieces on. Do you have anything but bone inside your skull?"

"Take your nosepiece off, then," said David, "and I'll take mine off. Stop me in fair fight, if you can."

"Fair fight!" came the approving shout from the

crowd, and Bigman yelled, "Put up or back down, Griswold." He leaped forward, ripping Griswold's blaster from his hip.

David put his hand to his nosepiece. "Ready?"

Bigman called, "I'll count three."

The men yelled confusedly. They were waiting now, in keen anticipation. Griswold glanced wildly about him.

Bigman was counting, "One——"

And at the count of "Three" David quietly removed his nosepiece, and tossed it, with the attached cylinders, to one side. He stood there, unprotected, holding his breath against the unbreathable atmosphere of Mars.

★ ★ ★ ★ Chapter 7

BIGMAN MAKES A DISCOVERY

Griswold did not stir, and his nosepiece remained in place. There was a threatening growl from the spectators.

David moved as quickly as he dared, gauging his steps against the light gravity. He lunged clumsily (it was almost as though water were holding him up) and caught Griswold about the shoulder. He twisted sideways, avoiding the farmboy's knee. One hand reached to Griswold's chin, caught the nosepiece and yanked it up and off.

Griswold grabbed for it with the beginning of a thin yell, but caught himself and clamped his mouth shut against the loss of any air. He broke away, staggering a bit. Slowly he circled David.

Nearly a minute had passed since David had drawn his last breath. His lungs felt the strain. Griswold, eyes bloodshot, crouched and sidled toward David. His legs were springy, his motions graceful. He was used to low gravity and could handle himself. David realized grimly that he himself probably could not. One quick, injudicious move and he might find himself sprawling.

Each second took its strain. David kept out of reach and watched the twisting grimace on Griswold's face tauten and grow tortured. He would have to outwait the farmboy. He himself had an athlete's lungs. Griswold ate too much and drank too much to be in proper shape. The fissure caught his eye. It was some four feet behind him now, a sheer cliff, dropping perpendicularly. It was toward it that Griswold was maneuvering him.

He halted his retreat. In ten seconds Griswold would have to charge. He would have to.

And Griswold did.

David let himself drop to one side, and caught the other with his shoulder. He whirled under the impact and allowed the force of the whirl to add itself to his own thrusting fist which caught Griswold's jawbone at its socket.

Griswold staggered blindly. He let out his breath in a huge puff and filled his lungs with a mixture of argon, neon, and carbon dioxide. Slowly, dreadfully, he crumpled. With a last effort he tried to raise himself, half succeeded, started falling again, tottered forward in an attempt to maintain his balance——

There was a confused yelling in David's ears. On trembling legs, deaf and blind to everything but his nose-piece on the ground, he walked back to the car. Forcing

78

his tortured, oxygen-craving body to work slowly and with dignity, he buckled on his cylinders with care and adjusted his nosepiece. Then, finally, he took a shuddering drag of oxygen that poured into his lungs like the rush of cold water into a desiccated stomach.

It was a full minute before he could do anything but breathe, his huge chest rising and falling in large, rapid sweeps. He opened his eyes.

"Where's Griswold?"

They were around him, all of them; Bigman in the very fore.

Bigman looked surprised. "Didn't you see?"

"I knocked him down." David looked about sharply. Griswold was nowhere.

Bigman made a down-sweeping motion with his hand. "Into the fissure."

"What?" David frowned beneath the nosepiece. "This is a bad joke."

"No, no." "Over the edge like a diver." "By Space, it was his own fault." "Clear case of self-defense for you, Earthie." They were all talking at once.

David said, "Wait, what happened? Did *I* throw him over?"

"No, Earthie," Bigman clamored. "It wasn't your doing. You hit him and the bug went down. Then he tried to get up. He started going down again, and when he tried to keep his balance, he sort of hopped forward, too blind to see what lay ahead of him. We tried to get him, but there wasn't enough time, and over he went. If he hadn't been so busy maneuvering you to the edge of the fissure so he could throw you over, it wouldn't have happened."

David looked at the men. They looked at him.

Finally one of the farmboys thrust out a hard hand. "Good show, farmboy."

It was calmly said, but it meant acceptance, and it broke the log jam.

Bigman yelled a triumph, jumped six feet into the air, and sank slowly down, with legs twiddling under him in a maneuver no ballet dancer, however expert, could have duplicated under Earth gravity. The others were crowding close now. Men who had addressed David only as "Earthie" or "You," or not at all, were clapping him on the back and telling him he was a man Mars could be proud of.

Bigman shouted, "Men, let's continue the checkup. Do we need Griswold to show us how?"

They howled back, "No!"

"Then how about it?" He vaulted into his car.

"Come on, farmboy," they yelled at David, who jumped into what had been Griswold's car fifteen minutes before and set it in motion.

Once again the call of "Sand awa-a-a-ay!" shrilled and ululated through the Martian wisps.

The news spread by sand-car radio, leaping across the empty spaces between the glass-enclosed stretches of farm lands. While David maneuvered his vehicle up and down the corridors between the glass walls, word of

Griswold's end made its way across all the expanse of the farm.

The eight remaining farmboys of what had been Griswold's sub-section gathered together once again in the dying ruddy light of Mars's sinking sun and retraced the early-morning drive back to the farm dome. When David returned, he found himself already notorious.

There was no formal evening meal that day. It had been eaten out in the desert before the return, so in less than half an hour of the completion of the checkup, men had gathered before the Main House, waiting.

There was no doubt that by now Hennes and the Old Man himself had heard of the fight. There were enough of the "Hennes crowd," that is, men who had been hired since Hennes had become foreman and whose interests were tied thoroughly to those of Hennes, to insure the fact that the news had spread in that direction. So the men waited with pleased anticipation.

It was not that they had any great hate for Hennes. He was efficient and no brute. But he was not liked. He was cold and aloof, lacked the quality of easy mixing which had marked earlier foremen. On Mars, with its lack of social distinctions, that was a serious shortcoming and one which the men could not help but resent. And Griswold himself had been anything but popular.

All in all, it was more excitement than the Makian farm had seen in three Martian years, and a Martian year is just one month short of being two Earth-years long.

When David appeared, a considerable cheer went up and way was made for him, though a small group well to one side looked glum and hostile.

Inside, the cheers must have been heard, for Makian, Hennes, Benson, and a few others stepped out. David walked up the foot of the ramp which led to the doorway and Hennes moved forward to the head of the ramp, where he stood, looking down.

David said, "Sir, I have come to explain today's incident."

Hennes said evenly, "A valuable employee of the Makian farms died today as the result of a quarrel with you. Can your explanation remove that fact?"

"No, sir, but the man Griswold was beaten in fair fight."

A voice called out from the crowd, "Griswold tried to kill the boy. He forgot to have the weight-rods included in the boy's car by *accident*." There were several scattered squawks of laughter at the final sarcastic word.

Hennes paled. His fists clenched. "Who said that?"

There was silence, and then from the very front of the crowd a small, subdued voice said, "Please, teacher, it wasn't I." Bigman was standing there, hands clasped before him, eyes looking modestly down.

The laughter came again, and this time it was a roar.

Hennes suppressed fury with an effort. He said to David, "Do you claim an attempt on your life?"

David said, "No, sir. I claim only a fair fight, witnessed by seven farmboys. A man who enters a fair fight must be willing to come out as best he can. Do you intend to set up new rules?"

A yell of approval went up from the audience. Hennes looked about him. He cried, "I am sorry that you men are being misled and agitated into actions you will regret. Now get back to your work, all of you, and be assured that your attitude this evening will not be forgotten. As for you, Williams, we will consider the case. This is not the end."

He slammed back into Main House and, after a moment's hesitation, the rest followed him.

David was called to Benson's office early the next day. It had been a long night of celebration, which David could neither avoid nor break away from, and he yawned prodigiously as he stooped to avoid hitting the lintel.

Benson said, "Come in, Williams." He was dressed in a white smock and the air in the office had a characteristic animal odor that came from the cages of rats and hamsters. He smiled. "You look sleepy. Sit down."

"Thanks," said David. "I *am* sleepy. What can I do for you?"

"It's what I can do for you, Williams. You're in trouble and you could be in worse trouble. I'm afraid you don't know what conditions on Mars are like. Mr. Makian has the full legal authority to order you blasted if he believes the death of Griswold can be considered murder."

"Without a trial?"

"No, but Hennes could find twelve farmboys who would think his way easily enough."

"He'd have trouble with the rest of the farmboys if he tried to do that, wouldn't he?"

"I know. I told Hennes that over and over again last night. Don't think that Hennes and I get along. He's too dictatorial for me; too fond, by far, of his own ideas, such as that private detective work of his which I mentioned to you the other time. And Mr. Makian agreed with me completely. He must let Hennes take charge of all direct dealings with the men, of course, which is why he didn't interfere yesterday, but he told Hennes afterward, to his face, that he wasn't going to sit by and see his farm destroyed over a stupid rascal such as Griswold, and Hennes had to promise to let the matter stew for a while. Just the same, he won't forget this in a hurry, and Hennes is a bad enemy to have here."

"I'll have to risk it, won't I?"

"We can run the risk to a minimum. I've asked Makian if I may use you here. You could be quite useful, you know, even without scientific training. You can help feed the animals and clean the cages. I could teach you how to anesthetize them and make injections. It won't be much, but it will keep you out of Hennes' way and prevent disruption of farm morale which is something we can't afford now, as you should know. Are you willing?"

With the utmost gravity David said, "It would be rather a social comedown for a man who's been told he's an honest-to-goodness farmboy now."

The scientist frowned. "Oh, come now, Williams. Don't take seriously what those fools tell you. Farmboy! Huh! It's a fancy name for a semi-skilled agricultural laborer and nothing more. You'd be silly to listen to their upside-down notions of social status. Look, if you work with me you might be helping to work out the mystery of the poisonings; help avenge your sister. That's why you came to Mars, wasn't it?"

"I'll work for you," said David.

"Good." Benson's round face stretched in a smile of relief.

Bigman looked through the door cautiously. He half whispered, "Hey!"

David turned around and closed the cage door. "Hello, Bigman."

"Is Benson around?"

"No. He's gone for the day."

"Okay." Bigman entered, walking carefully, as though to prevent even an accidental contact between his clothing and any object in the laboratories.

"Don't tell me you have something against Benson."

"Who, me? No. He's just a bit—you know." He tapped his temple a few times. "What kind of a grown man would come to Mars to fool around with little animals? And then he's always telling us how to run the planting and harvesting. What does he know? You can't learn anything about Mars farming in some Earth college. At that, he tries to make himself seem better than we are. You know what I mean? We have to slap him down sometimes."

He looked gloomily at David. "And now look at you. He's got you all spiffed out in a nightgown, too, playing nursemaid to a mouse. Why do you let him?"

"It's just for a while," said David.

"Well." Bigman pondered a moment, then thrust out his hand awkwardly. "I want to say good-by."

David took it. "Leaving?"

"My month's up. I have my papers so now I'll be getting a job somewhere else. I'm glad I met up with you, Earthie. Maybe when your own time's up we can meet again. You won't want to stay under Hennes."

"Hold on." David did not release the little fellow's hand. "You'll be going to Wingrad City now, won't you?"

"Till I find a job. Yes."

"Good. I've been waiting for this for a week. I can't leave the farm, Bigman, so will you do an errand for me?"

"You bet. Just name it."

"It's a little risky. You'd have to come back here."

"All right. I'm not afraid of Hennes. Besides, there are ways for us to meet he doesn't know a thing about. I've been on Makian farms a lot longer than he has."

David forced Bigman into a seat. He squatted next to him, and his voice was a whisper. "Look, there's a library at the corner of Canal and Phobos streets in Wingrad City. I want you to get some book films for me along with a viewer. The information that will get you the proper films is in this sealed——"

Bigman's hand clawed out sharply, seizing David's right sleeve, forcing it upward.

"Here, what are you doing?" demanded David.

"I want to see something," panted Bigman. He had bared David's wrist now, holding it, inner surface upward, watching it breathlessly.

David made no move to withdraw it. He watched his own wrist without concern. "Well, what's the idea?"

"Wrong one," muttered Bigman.

"Really?" David took his wrist away from Bigman's clutch effortlessly and exposed the other wrist. He held them both before him. "What are you looking for?"

"You know what I'm looking for. I thought your face was familiar ever since you came here. Couldn't place it. I could kick myself. What kind of an Earthman would come here and be rated as good as any native farmboy in less than a month? And I have to wait for you to send me to the library at the Council of Science before I tumble."

"I still don't understand you, Bigman."

"I think you do, David Starr." He nearly shouted the name in his triumph.

★ ★ ★ ★ Chapter 8

NIGHT MEETING

David said, "Quiet, man!"

Bigman's voice sank. "I've seen you in video reels often enough. But why don't your wrists show the mark? I've heard all members of the Council were marked."

"Where did you hear this? And who told you the library at Canal and Phobos is the Council of Science?"

Bigman flushed. "Don't look down at the farmboy, mister. I've lived in the city. I've even had schooling."

"My apologies. I didn't mean it that way. Will you still help me?"

"Not until I understand about your wrists."

"That's not hard. It's a colorless tattoo that will turn dark in air, but only if I want it to."

"How's that?"

"It's a matter of emotion. Each human emotion is

accompanied by a particular hormone pattern in the blood. One and only one such pattern activates the tattoo. I happen to know the emotion that fits."

David did nothing visibly, but slowly a patch on the inner surface of his right wrist appeared and darkened. The golden dots of the Big Dipper and Orion glowed momentarily and then the whole faded rapidly.

Bigman's face glowed and his hands came down for that automatic smack against his boots. David caught his arms roughly.

"Hey," said Bigman.

"No excitement, please. Are you with me?"

"Sure I'm with you. I'll be back tonight with the stuff you want and I'll tell you where we can meet. There's a place outside, near the Second Section——" He went on, whispering directions.

David nodded. "Good. Here's the envelope."

Bigman took it and inserted it between his hip boot and thigh. He said, "There's a pocket on the inside top of the better-quality hip boots, Mr. Starr. Do you know that?"

"I do. Don't look down at this farmboy, either. And my name, Bigman, is still Williams. That leaves just one last statement. The Council librarians will be the only ones who will be able to open that envelope safely. If anyone else tries, he'll be hurt."

Bigman drew himself up. "No one else will open it. There are people who are bigger than I am. Maybe you think I don't know that, but I do. Just the same, bigger or not, nobody, and I mean nobody, will take this from me without killing me. What's more, I wasn't thinking of opening it myself, either, if you've given that any thought."

"I have," said David. "I try to give all possibilities some thought, but I didn't give that one very much."

Bigman smiled, made a mock pass with his fist at David's chin, and was gone.

It was almost dinnertime when Benson returned. He looked unhappy and his plump cheeks were drooping.

He said listlessly, "How are you, Williams?"

David was washing his hands by dipping them into the special detergent solution which was universally used on Mars for this purpose. He withdrew his hands into the stream of warm air for drying, while the wash water flushed away into the tanks where it could be purified and returned to the central supply. Water was expensive on Mars and was used and reused wherever possible.

David said, "You look tired, Mr. Benson."

Benson closed the door carefully behind him. He blurted it out. "Six people died yesterday of the poisoning. That's the highest number yet for a single day. It's getting worse all the time and there's nothing we seem to be able to do."

He glowered at the lines of animal cages. "All alive, I suppose."

"All alive," said David.

"Well, what can I do? Every day Makian asks me if I have discovered anything. Does he think I can find discoveries under my pillow in the morning? I was in the grain bins today, Williams. It was an ocean of wheat, thousands and thousands of tons all set for shipment to Earth. I dipped into it a hundred times. Fifty grains here; fifty grains there. I tried every corner of every bin. I had them dip twenty feet down for samples. But what good is it? Under present conditions it would be a generous estimate to suppose that one out of a billion grains is infected."

He nudged at the suitcase he had brought with him. "Do you think the fifty thousand grains I've got here have the one in a billion among them? One chance in twenty thousand!"

David said, "Mr. Benson, you told me that no one ever died on the farm here, even though we eat Martian food almost exclusively."

"Not as far as I know."

"How about Mars as a whole?"

Benson frowned. "I don't know. I suppose not or I would have heard of it. Of course life isn't as tightly organized here on Mars as it is on Earth. A farmboy dies and usually he is simply buried without formality. There are few questions." Then, sharply, "Why do you ask?"

"I was just thinking that if it were a Martian germ, people on Mars might be more accustomed to it than Earth people. They might be immune."

"Well! Not a bad thought for a non-scientist. In fact, it's a good idea. I'll keep it in mind." He reached up to pat David's shoulder. "You go on and eat. We'll begin feeding the new samples tomorrow."

As David left, Benson turned to his suitcase and was lifting out the carefully labeled little packets, one of which might hold the all-important poisoned kernel. By tomorrow those samples would be ground, each little pile of powder carefully mixed and painstakingly divided into twenty sub-samples, some for feeding and some for testing.

By tomorrow! David smiled tightly to himself. He wondered where he would be tomorrow. He even wondered if he would be alive tomorrow.

The farm dome lay asleep like a giant prehistoric monster curled upon the surface of Mars. The residual fluorescents were pale glimmers against the dome roof. Amid the silence the ordinarily unheard vibrations of the dome's atmospherics, which compressed Martian atmosphere to the normal Earth level and added moisture and oxygen from the quantities supplied by the growing plants of the vast greenhouses, sounded in a low grumble.

David was moving quickly from shadow to shadow with a caution that was, to a large extent, not necessary. There was no one watching. The hard composition of the dome was low overhead, bending rapidly to the ground, when he reached Lock 17. His hair brushed it.

The inner door was open and he stepped inside. His pencil flashlight swept the walls within and found the controls. They weren't labeled, but Bigman's directions had been clear enough. He depressed the yellow button. There was a faint click, a pause, and then the soughing of air. It was much louder than it had been on the day of the checkup, and since the lock was a small one designed for three or four men rather than a giant one designed for nine sand-cars, the air pressure dropped much more quickly.

He adjusted his nosepiece, waited for the hissing to die away, the silence indicating pressure equilibrium. Only then did he depress the red button. The outer section lifted and he stepped out.

This time he was not trying to control a car. He lowered himself to the hard, cold sands and waited for the stomach-turning sensations to pass as he accustomed himself to the gravity change. It took scarcely two minutes for that to happen. A few more gravity-change passages, David thought grimly, and he would have what the farmboys called "gravity legs."

He rose, turned to get his bearings, and then found himself, quite involuntarily, frozen in fascination!

It was the first time he had ever seen the Martian night sky. The stars themselves were the old familiar ones of Earth, arranged in all the familiar constellations. The distance from Mars to Earth, great though it was, was insufficient to alter perceptibly the relative positions of the distant stars. But though the stars were unchanged in position, how vastly they were changed in brilliance.

The thinner air of Mars scarcely softened them, but left them hard and gem-bright. There was no moon, of course, not one such as Earth knew. Mars's two satellites, Phobos and Deimos, were tiny things only five or ten miles across, simply mountains flying loose in space. Even though they were much closer to Mars than the

Moon was to Earth, they would show no disk and be only two more stars.

He searched for them, even though he realized they might easily both be on the other side of Mars. Low on the western horizon he caught something else. Slowly he turned to it. It was by far the brightest object in the sky, with a faint blue-green tinge to it that was matched for beauty by nothing else in the heavens he watched. Separated from it by about the width of Mars's shrunken sun was another object, yellower, bright in itself but dwarfed by the much greater brilliance of its neighbor.

David needed no star map to identify the double object. They were the Earth and the Moon, the double "evening star" of Mars.

He tore his eyes away, turned toward the low outcropping of rock visible in the light of his pencil flash, and began walking. Bigman had told him to use those rocks as a guide. It was cold in the Martian night, and David was regretfully aware of the heating powers of even the Martian sun, one hundred and thirty million miles away.

The sand-car was invisible, or nearly so, in the weak starlight, and he heard the low, even purr of its engines long before he saw it.

He called, "Bigman!" and the little fellow popped out of it.

"Space!" said Bigman. "I was beginning to think you were lost."

"Why is the engine running?"

"That's easy. How else do I keep from freezing to

death? We won't be heard, though. I know this place."

"Do you have the films?"

"*Do* I? Listen, I don't know what you had in the message you sent but they had five or six scholars circling me like satellites. It was 'Mr. Jones this' and 'Mr. Jones that.' I said, 'My name's Bigman,' I said. And then it was 'Mr. Bigman, if you please.' Anyway"—Bigman ticked items off on his fingers—"before the day was gone, they had four films for me, two viewers, a box as big as myself which I haven't opened, and the loan (or maybe the gift for all I know) of a sand-car to carry it all in."

David smiled but made no answer. He entered into the welcome warmth of the car and quickly, in a race to outrun the fleet night, adjusted the viewers for projection and inserted a film in each. Direct viewing would have been quicker, more preferable, but even in the warm interior of the sand-car his nosepiece was still a necessity, and the bulbous transparent covering of his eyes made direct viewing impossible.

Slowly the sand-car lurched forward through the night, repeating almost exactly the route of Griswold's subsection on the day of the checkup.

"I don't get it," said Bigman. He had been muttering under his breath uselessly for fifteen minutes and now he had to repeat his louder statement twice before the brooding David would respond.

"Don't get what?"

"What you're doing. Where you're going. I figure this is my business because I'm going to stay with you from here on. I've been thinking today, Mr. St—Williams, thinking a lot. Mr. Makian's been in a kind of biting temper for months now, and he wasn't a bad joe at all before that. Hennes came in at that time, with a new shuffle for all hands. And Schoolboy Benson gets *his* licks in all of a sudden. Before it all started he was nobody, and now he's real pally with the big shots. Then, to top it off, you're here, with the Council of Science ready to put up anything you want. It's something big, I know, and I want to be in on it."

"Do you?" said David. "Did you see the maps I was viewing?"

"Sure. Just old maps of Mars. I've seen them a million times."

"How about the ones with the crosshatched areas? Do you know what those areas stood for?"

"Any farmboy can tell you that. There are supposed to be caverns underneath, except that I don't believe it. My point is this. How in Space can anyone tell there are holes two miles underneath the ground if no one's been down there to see? Tell me that."

David did not bother to describe the science of seismography to Bigman. Instead, he said, "Ever hear of Martians?"

Bigman began, "Sure. What kind of a question——" and then the sand-car screeched and trembled as the little fellow's hands moved convulsively on the wheels. "You mean *real* Martians? *Mars* Martians; not *people* Martians like us? Martians living here before people came?"

His thin laugh rattled piercingly inside the car and when he caught his breath again (it is difficult to laugh and breathe at the same time with a nosepiece on), he said, "You've been talking to that guy Benson."

David remained gravely unruffled at the other's glee. "Why do you say that, Bigman?"

"We once caught him reading some kind of book about it, and we ribbed the pants off him. Jumping Asteroids, he got sore. He called us all ignorant peasants, and I looked up the word in the dictionary and told the boys what it meant. There was talk of mayhem for a while, and he got shoved around sort of by accident, if you know what I mean, for a while after that. He never mentioned anything about Martians to *us* after that; wouldn't have had the nerve. I guess, though, he figured you were an Earthman and would fall for that kind of comet gas."

"Are you sure it's comet gas?"

"Sure. What else can it be? People have been on Mars for hundreds and hundreds of years. No one's ever seen Martians."

"Suppose they're down in the caverns two miles underneath."

"No one's seen the caverns either. Besides, how would the Martians get there in the first place? People have been over every inch of Mars and there sure aren't staircases going down anywhere. Or elevators, either."

"Are you certain? I saw one the other day."

"What?" Bigman looked back over his shoulder. He said, "Kidding me?"

"It wasn't a staircase, but it was a hole. And it was at *least* two miles deep."

"Oh, you mean the *fissure*. Nuts, that doesn't mean anything. Mars is full of fissures."

"Exactly, Bigman. And I've got detailed maps of the fissures on Mars too. Right here. There's a funny thing about them which, as nearly as I can tell from the geography you brought me, hasn't been noticed before. Not a single fissure crosses a single cavern."

"What does that prove?"

"It makes sense. If you were building airtight caverns, would you want a hole in the roof? And there's another coincidence. Each fissure cuts close to a cavern, but without ever touching, as though the Martians used them as points of entrance into the caverns they were building."

The sand-car stopped suddenly. In the dim light of the viewers, which were still focused on two maps projected simultaneously upon the flat white surface of the built-in screens, Bigman's face blinked somberly at David in the back seat.

He said, "Wait a minute. Wait a jumping minute. Where are we going?"

"To the fissure, Bigman. About two miles past the place where Griswold went over. That's where it gets nearest the cavern under the Makian farms."

"And once we get there?"

David said calmly, "Once we get there, why, I'll climb down into it."

Chapter 9

INTO THE FISSURE

"Are you serious?" asked Bigman.

"Quite serious," said David.

"You mean"—he tried to smile—"there really *are* Martians?"

"Would you believe me if I said there were?"

"No." He came to a sudden decision. "But that doesn't matter. I said I wanted to be in this, and I don't back out." Once again the car moved forward.

The feeble dawn of the Martian heavens was beginning to light the grim landscape when the car approached the fissure. It had been creeping for half an hour previous, its powerful headlights probing the darkness, lest, as Bigman had put it, they find the fissure a little too quickly.

David climbed out of the car and approached the giant crack. No light penetrated it as yet. It was a black and ominous hole in the ground, stretching out of sight in

99

either direction, with the opposing lip a featureless gray prominence. He pointed his flash downward and the beam of light faded into nothing.

Bigman came up behind him. "Are you sure this is the right place?"

David looked about him. "According to the maps, this is the closest approach to a cavern. How far are we from the nearest farm section?"

"Two miles easy."

The Earthman nodded. Farmboys were unlikely to touch this spot except possibly during checkup.

He said, "No use waiting then."

Bigman said, "How are you going to do it, anyway?"

David had already lifted the box which Bigman had obtained in Wingrad City out of the car. He tore it open and took out the contents. "Ever see one of these?" he asked.

Bigman shook his head. He twiddled a piece of it between gloved thumb and forefinger. It consisted of a pair of long ropes with a silky sheen connected at twelve-inch intervals by crosspieces.

"It's a rope ladder, I suppose," he said.

"Yes," said David, "but not rope. This is spun silicone, lighter than magnesium, stronger than steel, and barely affected by any temperatures we're likely to meet on Mars. Mostly, it's used on the Moon, where the gravity is really low and the mountains really high. On Mars, there's not much use for it because it's a rather flat world. In fact, it was a stroke of luck that the Council could locate one in the city."

"What good will this do you?" Bigman was running the length of it through his hands until the ladder ended in a thick bulb of metal.

"Careful," said David. "If the safety catch isn't on, you can damage yourself pretty badly."

He took it gently out of Bigman's hand, encircled the metal bulb with his own strong hands, and twisted each hand in opposing directions. There was a sharp little click, but when he released his hold, the bulb seemed unchanged.

"Now look." The soil of Mars thinned and vanished at the approaches of the fissure, and the cliff edge was naked rock. David bent and, with a light pressure, touched the bulb end of the ladder to the crag, faintly ruddy in the flushing sky of morning. He took his hand away, and it remained there, balanced at an odd angle.

"Lift it up," he said.

Bigman looked at him, bent, and lifted. For a moment he looked puzzled as the bulb remained where it was; then he yanked with all his might and still nothing happened.

He looked up angrily. "What did you do?"

David smiled. "When the safety is released, any pressure at the tip of the bulb releases a thin force-field about twelve inches long that cuts right into the rock. The end of the field then expands outward in each direction about six inches, to make a 'T' of force. The limits of the field are blunt, not sharp, so you can't loosen it by yanking it from side to side. The only way you can pull out the bulb is to break the rock clean off."

"How do you release it?"

David ran the hundred-foot length of ladder through his hands and came up with a similar bulb at the other end. He twisted it, then pushed it at the rock. It remained there, and after some fifteen seconds the first bulb fell on its side.

"If you activate one bulb," he said, "the other is automatically deactivated. Or, of course, if you adjust the safety catch of an activated bulb"—he bent down and did so—"it is deactivated"—he lifted it up—"and the other remains unaffected."

Bigman squatted. Where the two bulbs had been there were now narrow cuts about four inches long in the living rock. They were too narrow for him to insert his fingernail.

David Starr was speaking. He said, "I've got water and food for a week. I'm afraid my oxygen won't last more than two days, but you wait a week anyway. If I'm not back then, this is the letter you're to deliver to the Council headquarters."

"Hold on. You don't really think these fairy-tale Martians——"

"I mean lots of things. I mean I may slip. The rope ladder may be faulty. I may accidentally anchor it to a point at which there is a fault in the rock. Anything. So can I rely on you?"

Bigman looked disappointed. "But that's a fine situation. Am I supposed to sit around up here while you take all the risks?"

"It's the way a team works, Bigman. You know that."

He was stooping at the lip of the fissure. The sun was edging over the horizon before them and the sky had faded from black to purple. The fissure, however, remained a forbidding dusky abyss. The sparse atmosphere of Mars did not scatter light very well, and only when the sun was directly overhead was the eternal night of the fissure dispelled.

Stolidly David tossed the ladder into the fissure. Its fiber made no noise as it swung against the rock, upheld by the knob which held tightly to the stony lip. A hundred feet below they could hear the other knob thump once or twice.

David yanked at the rope to test its hold, then, seizing the topmost rung with his hands, he vaulted into the abyss himself. It was a feathery feeling floating down at less than half the speed one would have on Earth, but there it ended. His actual weight was not far below Earth normal, considering the two oxygen cylinders he carried, each the largest size available at the farm.

His head projected above surface. Bigman was staring at him, wide-eyed. David said, "Now get away and take the car with you. Return the films and viewers to the Council and leave the scooter."

"Right," said Bigman. All cars carried emergency four-wheeled platforms that could travel fifty miles under their own power. They were uncomfortable and no protection at all against cold or, worse still, against dust storms Still, when a sand-car broke down miles from home, scooters were better than waiting to be found.

David Starr looked downward. It was too dark to see the end of the ladder, the sheen of which glimmered into grayness. Allowing his legs to dangle free, he scrambled down the face of the cliff rung by rung, counting as he did so. At the eightieth rung he reached for the free end of the ladder and reeled it in after hooking an arm about and through a rung, leaving both hands free.

When the lower bulb was in his hand, he reached to the right and thrust it at the face of the cliff. It remained there. He yanked hard at it, and it held. Quickly he swung himself from his previous position to the branch of the rope ladder now dangling from the new anchor. One hand remained on the portion of the ladder he had left, waiting for it to give. When it did so, he swung it outward, so that the bulb from above would swing wide of himself as it fell.

He felt a slight pendulum effect upon himself as the bulb, which had been at the lip of the fissure thirty seconds before, now lashed back and forth some one hundred and eighty feet below the surface of Mars. He looked up. There was a broad swath of purple sky to be seen, but he knew it would get narrower and narrower with each rung he descended.

Down he went, and at every eighty rungs he set himself a new anchor, first to the right of the old one and then to the left, maintaining in general a straight passage downward.

Six hours had passed, and once again David paused for a bite of concentrated ration and a swig of water from his canteen. Catching his feet in rungs and relaxing the pressure on his arms was all he could do in the way of resting. Nowhere in all the descent had there been a horizontal ledge large enough for him to catch his breath upon. At least nowhere within the reach of his flashlight.

That was bad in other ways. It meant that the trip upward, supposing that there ever was to be a trip upward, would have to be made by the slow method of jabbing each bulb, in turn, at a spot as high as one could reach. It could be done and had been—on the Moon. On Mars the gravity was more than twice what it was on the Moon, and progress would be horribly slow, far slower than the journey down was. And that, David realized grimly, was slow enough. He could not be much more than a mile below surface.

Downward there was only black. Above, the now narrow streak of sky had brightened. David decided to wait. It was past eleven by his Earth-time watch, and that had fair significance on Mars, where the period of rotation was only half an hour longer than on Earth. The sun would soon be overhead.

He thought soberly that the maps of the Martian caverns were at best only rough approximations from the action of vibration waves under the planet's surface. With very slight errors existing he could be miles away from the true entrance into the caverns.

And then, too, there might be no entrances at all. The caverns might be purely natural phenomena, like the

Carlsbad Caverns on Earth. Except, of course, that these Martian caverns were hundreds of miles across.

He waited, almost drowsily, hanging loosely over nothing, in darkness and silence. He flexed his numbed fingers. Even under the gloves, the Martian cold nipped. When he was descending, the activity kept him warm; when he waited, the cold burrowed in.

He had almost decided to renew his climbing to keep from freezing when he caught the first approach of dim light. He looked up and saw the slowly descending dim yellow of sunlight. Over the lip of the fissure, into the small streak of sky that remained to his vision, the sun came. It took ten minutes for the light to increase to maximum, when the entire burning globe had become visible. Small though it was to an Earthman's eyes, its width was one quarter that of the fissure opening. David knew the light would last half an hour or less and that the darkness would return for twenty-four hours thereafter.

He looked about rapidly, swinging as he did so. The wall of the fissure was by no means straight. It was jagged, but it was everywhere vertical. It was as though a cut had been made into the Martian soil with a badly crimped knife, but one which cut straight down. The opposite wall was considerably closer than it had been at the surface, but David estimated that there would be at least another mile or two of descent before it would be close enough to touch.

Still, it all amounted to nothing. Nothing!

And then he saw the patch of blackness. David's breath

whistled sharply. There was considerable blackness elsewhere. Wherever an outcropping of rock cast a shadow,
there was blackness. It was just that this particular patch
was rectangular. It had perfect, or what seemed to be
perfect, right angles. It *had* to be artificial. It was like a
door of some sort set into the rock.

Quickly he caught up the lower knob of the ladder,
set it as far out in the direction of the patch as he could
reach, gathered in the other knob as it fell, and set it
still farther out in the same direction. He alternated them
as rapidly as he could, hoping savagely that the sun
would hold out, that the patch itself was not, somehow,
an illusion.

The sun had crossed the fissure and now touched the
lip of the wall from which he dangled. The rock he
faced, which had been yellow-red, turned gray again.
But there was still light upon the other wall, and he
could see well enough. He was less than a hundred feet
away, and each alternation of ladder knobs brought him
a yard closer.

Glimmering, the sunlight traveled up the opposite
wall, and the dusk was closing in when he reached the
edge of the patch. His gloved fingers closed upon the
edge of a cavity set into the rock. *It was smooth.* The
line had neither fault nor flaw. It *had* to be made by
intelligence.

He needed sunlight no longer. The small beam of the
flashlight would be enough. He swung his ladder into
the inset, and when he dropped a knob he felt it clunk
sharply on rock beneath. A horizontal ledge!

He descended quickly, and in a few minutes found himself standing on rock. For the first time in more than six hours he was standing on something solid. He found the inactive bulb, thrust it into rock at waist level, brought down the ladder, then adjusted the safety latch and pulled out the bulb. For the first time in more than six hours both ends of the ladder were free.

David looped the ladder around his waist and arm and looked about. The cavity in the face of the cliff was about ten feet high and six across. With his flashlight pointing the way, he walked inward and came face to face with a smooth and quite solid stone slab that barred farther progress.

It, too, was the work of intelligence. It had to be. But it remained an effective barrier to further exploration just the same.

There was a sudden pain in his ears, and he spun sharply. There could be only one explanation. Somehow the air pressure about himself was increasing. He moved back toward the face of the cliff and was not surprised to find that the opening through which he had come was barred by rock which had not previously been there. It had slid into place without a sound.

His heart beat quickly. He was obviously in an air lock of some sort. Carefully he removed his nosepiece and sampled the new air. It felt good in his lungs, and it was warm.

He advanced to the inner slab of rock and waited confidently for it to lift up and away.

It did exactly that, but a full minute before it did so

David felt his arms compressed suddenly against his body as though a steel lasso had been thrown about him and tightened. He had time for one startled cry, and then his legs pushed one against the other under similar pressure.

And so it was that when the inner door opened and the way to enter the cavern was clear before him, David Starr could move neither hand nor foot.

★ ★ ★ ★ Chapter 10

BIRTH OF THE SPACE RANGER

David waited. There was no use in speaking to empty air. Presumably the entities who had built the caverns and who could so immobilize him in so immaterial a fashion would be perfectly capable of playing all the cards.

He felt himself lift from the ground and slowly tip backward until the line of his body was parallel with the floor. He tried to crane his head upward but found it to be nearly immovable. The bonds were not so strong as those which had tightened about his limbs. It was rather like a harness of velvety rubber that gave, but only so far.

He moved inward smoothly. It was like entering warm, fragrant, breathable water. As his head left the air lock, the last portion of his body to do so, a dreamless sleep closed over him.

David Starr opened his eyes with no sensation of any passage of time but, with the sensation of life near by. Exactly what form that sensation took he could not say. He was first conscious of the heat. It was that of a hot summer day on Earth. Second, there was the dim red light that surrounded him and that scarcely sufficed for vision. By it he could barely make out the walls of a small room as he turned his head. Nowhere was there motion; nowhere life.

And yet somewhere near there must be the working of a powerful intelligence. David felt that in a way he could not explain.

Cautiously he tried to move a hand, and it lifted without hindrance. Wonderingly he sat upright and found himself on a surface that yielded and gave but whose nature he could not make out in the dimness.

The voice came suddenly. "The creature is aware of its surroundings . . ." The last part of the statement was a jumble of meaningless sound. David could not identify the direction from which the voice came. It was from all directions and no direction.

A second voice sounded. It was different, though the difference was a subtle one. It was gentler, smoother, more feminine, somehow. "Are you well, creature?"

David said, "I cannot see you."

The first voice (David thought of it as a man's) sounded again. "It is then as I told . . ." Again the jumble. "You are not equipped to see mind."

The last phrase was blurred, but to David it sounded like "see mind."

"I can see matter," he said, "but there is scarcely light to see by."

There was a silence, as though the two were conferring apart, and then there was the gentle thrusting of an object into David's hand. It was his flashlight.

"Has this," came the masculine voice, "any significance to you with regard to light?"

"Why, certainly. Don't you see?" He flashed it on and quickly splashed the light beam about himself. The room *was* empty of life, and quite bare. The surface he rested upon was transparent to light and some four feet off the floor.

"It is as I said," said the feminine voice excitedly. "The creature's sight sense is activated by short-wave radiation."

"But most of the radiation of the instrument is in the infrared. It was that I judged by," protested the other. The light was brightening even as the voice sounded, turning first orange, then yellow, and finally white.

David said, "Can you cool the room too?"

"But it has been carefully adjusted to the temperature of your body."

"Nevertheless, I would have it cooler."

They were co-operative, at least. A cool wind swept over David, welcome and refreshing. He let the temperature drop to seventy before he stopped them.

David thought, "I think you are communicating directly with my mind. Presumably that is why I seem to hear you speaking International English."

The masculine voice said, "The last phrase is a jumble,

but certainly we are communicating. How else would that be done?"

David nodded to himself. That accounted for the occasional noisy blur. When a proper name was used that had no accompanying picture for his own mind to interpret, it could only be received as a blur. Mental static.

The feminine voice said, "In the early history of our race there are legends that our minds were closed to one another and that we communicated by means of symbols for the eye and ear. From your question I cannot help but wonder if this is the case with your own people, creature."

David said, "That is so. How long is it since I was brought into the cavern?"

The masculine voice said, "Not quite a planetary rotation. We apologize for any inconvenience we caused you, but it was our first opportunity to study one of the new surface creatures alive. We have salvaged several before this, one only a short while ago, but none were functional, and the amount of information obtained from such is, of necessity, limited."

David wondered if Griswold had been the recently salvaged corpse. He said cautiously, "Is your examination of myself over?"

The feminine voice responded quickly. "You fear harm. There is a distinct impression in your mind that we may be so savage as to interfere with your life functions in order to gain knowledge. How horrible!"

"I'm sorry if I have offended you. It is merely that I am unacquainted with your methods."

The masculine voice said, "We know all we need. We are quite capable of making a molecule-by-molecule investigation of your body without the need of physical contact at all. The evidence of our psycho-mechanisms is quite sufficient."

"What are these psycho-mechanisms you mention?"

"Are you acquainted with matter-mind transformations?"

"I am afraid not."

There was a pause, and then the masculine voice said curtly, "I have just investigated your mind. I am afraid, judging by its texture, that your grasp of scientific principles is insufficient for you to understand my explanations."

David felt put in his place. He said, "My apologies."

The masculine voice went on. "I would ask you some questions."

"Proceed, sir."

"What was the last part of your statement?"

"It was merely a manner of honorable address."

A pause. "Oh yes, I see. You complicate your communication symbols in accordance with the person you address. An odd custom. But I delay. Tell me, creature, you radiate an enormous heat. Are you ill or can this be normal?"

"It is quite normal. The dead bodies you examined were undoubtedly at the temperature of their environment, whatever it was. But while functioning, our bodies maintain a constant temperature that best suits us."

"Then you are not natives of this planet?"

BIRTH OF THE SPACE RANGER

David said, "Before I answer this question, may I ask you what your attitude would be toward creatures like myself if we originated from another planet?"

"I assure you that you and your fellow creatures are a matter of indifference to us except in so far as you arouse our curiosity. I see from your mind that you are uneasy with regard to our motives. I see that you fear our hostility. Remove such thoughts."

"Can you not read in my mind, then, the answer to your questions? Why do you question me specifically?"

"I can only read emotions and general attitudes in absence of precise communication. But, then, you are a creature and would not understand. For precise information, communication must involve an effort of will. If it will help to ease your mind, I will inform you that we have every reason to believe you to be a member of a race not native to this planet. For one thing, the composition of your tissues is utterly different from that of any living thing ever known to have existed on the face of the world. Your body heat indicates also that you come from another world, a warmer one."

"You are correct. We come from Earth."

"I do not understand the last word."

"From the planet next nearer the sun than this one."

"So! That is most interesting. At the time our race retired to the caverns some half a million revolutions ago we knew your planet to possess life, though probably not intelligence. Was your race intelligent then?"

"Scarcely," said David. One million Earth-years had

passed since the Martians had left the surface of their planet.

"It is indeed interesting. I must carry this report to the Central Mind directly. Come, ——."

"Let me remain behind, ——. I would like to communicate further with this creature."

"As you please."

The feminine voice said, "Tell me of your world."

David spoke freely. He felt a pleasant, almost delicious, languor. Suspicion departed and there was no reason he could not answer truthfully and in full. These beings were kind and friendly. He bubbled with information.

And then she released her hold on his mind and he stopped abruptly. Angrily he said, "What have I been saying?"

"Nothing of harm," the feminine voice assured him. "I have merely repressed the inhibitions of your mind. It is unlawful to do so, and I would not have dared do it if —— were here. But you are only a creature and I am so curious. I knew that your suspicion was too deep to let you talk without a little help from me and your suspicion is so misplaced. We would never harm you creatures as long as you do not intrude upon us."

"We have already done so, have we not?" asked David. "We occupy your planet from end to end."

"You are still testing me. You mistrust me. The surface of the planet is of no interest to us. *This* is home. And yet," the feminine voice seemed almost wistful, "there must be a certain thrill in traveling from world to world. We are well aware that there are many planets in space and many suns. To think that creatures like yourself are inheriting all that. It is all so interesting that I am thankful again and again that we sensed you making your clumsy way down toward us in time to make an opening for you."

"What!" David could not help but shout, although he knew that the sound waves his vocal cords created went unheeded and that only the thoughts of his mind were sensed. "You *made* that opening?"

"Not I alone. —— helped. That is why we were given the chance to investigate you."

"But how did you do it?"

"Why, by willing it."

"I don't understand."

"But it is simple. Can you not see it in my mind? But I forget. You are a creature. You see, when we retired to the caverns we were forced to destroy many thousands of cubic miles of matter to make space for ourselves under the surface. There was nowhere to store the matter as such, so we converted it to energy and —— —— —— ——."

"No, no, I don't follow you."

"You don't understand? In that case, all I can say is that the energy was stored in such a way that it could be tapped by an effort of the mind."

"But if all the matter that was once in these vast caverns were converted into energy——"

"There would be a great deal. Certainly. We have

lived on that energy for half a million revolutions, and it is calculated that we have enough for twenty million more revolutions. Even before we left the surface we had studied the relation of mind and matter and since we have come to the caverns we have perfected the science to such a degree that we have abandoned matter entirely as far as our personal use is concerned. We are creatures of pure mind and energy, who never die and are no longer born. I am here with you, but since you cannot sense mind, you are not aware of me except with your mind."

"But surely people such as yourselves can make themselves heir to all the universe."

"You fear that we shall contest the universe with poor material creatures such as yourself? That we shall fight for a place among the stars? That is silly. All the universe is here with us. We are sufficient to ourselves."

David was silent. Then slowly he put his hands to his head as he had the sensation of fine, very fine tendrils gently touching his mind. It was the first time the feeling had come, and he shrank from its intimacy.

She said, "My apologies again. But you are such an interesting creature. Your mind tells me that your fellow creatures are in great danger and you suspect that we might be the cause. I assure you, creature, it is not so."

She said it simply. David had no course but to believe.

He said, "Your companion said my tissue chemistry was entirely different from that of any life on Mars. May I ask how?"

"It is composed of a nitrogenous material."

"Protein," explained David.

"I do not understand that word."

"What are your tissues composed of?"

"Of —— —— ——. It is entirely different. There is practically no nitrogen in it."

"You could offer me no food, then?"

"I am afraid not. —— says any organic matter of our planet would be quickly poisonous to you. We could manufacture simple compounds of your life type that you might feed on, but the complex nitrogenous material that forms the bulk of your tissue is quite beyond us without much study. Are you hungry, creature?" There was no mistaking the sympathy and concern in her thoughts. (David persisted in thinking of it as a voice.)

He said, "For the moment I have still my own food."

The feminine voice said, "It seems unpleasant for me to think of you simply as a creature. What is your name?" Then, as though she feared she might not be understood, "How do your fellow creatures identify you?"

"I am called David Starr."

"I do not understand that except that there seems a reference to the suns of the universe. Do they call you that because you are a traveler through space?"

"No. Many of my people travel through space. 'Starr' has no particular meaning at present. It is simply a sound to identify me, as your names are simply sounds. At least they make no picture; I cannot understand them."

"What a pity. You should have a name which would

indicate your travels through space; the way in which you range from one end of the universe to the other. If I were a creature such as yourself, it seems to me that it would be fitting I should be called 'Space Ranger.' "

And so it was that from the lips of a living creature he did not see and could never see in its true form David Starr heard, for the first time, the name by which, eventually, all the Galaxy would know him.

★ ★ ★ ★ Chapter 11

THE STORM

A deeper, slower voice now took form in David's mind. It said gravely, "I greet you, creature. It is a good name ——— has just given you."

The feminine voice said, "I make way for you ——— ———."

By the loss of a faint touch upon his mind David became unmistakably aware that the owner of the feminine voice was no longer in mental contact. He turned warily, laboring once more under the illusion that there was direction to these voices and finding his untried mind still attempting to interpret in the old inadequate ways something with which it had never before come in contact. The voice came from no direction, of course. It was within his mind.

The creature of the deep voice gauged the difficulty. It said, "You are disturbed by the failure of your sense equipment to detect me and I do not wish you to be disturbed. I could adopt the outward physical appearance of a creature such as yourself but that would be a poor and undignified imposture. Will this suffice?"

David Starr watched the glimmer appear in the air before him. It was a soft streak of blue-green light about seven feet high and a foot wide.

He said calmly, "That is quite sufficient."

The deep voice said, "Good! And now let me explain who I am. I am the Administrator of —— ——. The report of the capture of a live specimen of the new surface life came to me as a matter of course. I will examine your mind."

The office of the new being had been a jumble of sound, and nothing more, to David, but he had caught the unmistakable sense of dignity and responsibility that accompanied it. Nevertheless he said firmly, "I would much prefer that you remained outside my mind."

"Your modesty," said the deep voice, "is quite understandable and praiseworthy. I should explain that my inspection would be confined most carefully to the outer fringes only. I would avoid very scrupulously any intrusion on your inner privacy."

David tensed his muscles uselessly. For long minutes there was nothing. Even the illusive feathery touch upon his mind, that had been present when the owner of the feminine voice had probed it, was absent from this new and more experienced inspection. And yet David was aware, without knowing how he could possibly be aware, of the compartments of his mind being delicately opened, then closed, without pain or disturbance.

The deep voice said, "I thank you. You will be released very shortly and returned to the surface."

David said defiantly, "What have you found in my mind?"

"Enough to pity your fellows. We of the Inner Life were once like yourselves so we have some comprehension of it. Your people are out of balance with the universe. You have a questioning mind that seeks to understand what it dimly senses, without possessing the truer, deeper senses that alone can reveal reality to you. In your futile seeking after the shadows that encompass you, you drive through space to the outermost limits of the Galaxy. It is as I have said; ——— has named you well. You are a race of Space Rangers indeed.

"Yet of what use is your ranging? The true victory is within. To understand the material universe, you must first become divorced from it as we are. We have turned away from the stars and toward ourselves. We have retreated to the caverns of our one world and abandoned our bodies. With us there is no longer death, except when a mind would rest; or birth, except when a mind gone to rest must be replaced."

David said, "Yet you are not all-sufficient to yourselves. Some of you suffer from curiosity. The being who spoke to me before wished to know of Earth."

"——— is recently born. Her days are not equal to a hundred revolutions of the planet about the sun. Her control of thought patterns is imperfect. We who are mature can easily conceive all the various designs into which your Earth history could have been woven. Few of them would be comprehensible to yourself, and not in an infinity of years could we have exhausted the thoughts possible in the consideration of your one world, and each thought would have been as fascinating and stimulating as the one thought which happens to represent reality. In time ——— will learn that this is so."

"Yet you yourself take the trouble to examine my mind."

"In order that I may make certain of that which I previously merely suspected. Your race has the capacity for growth. Under the best circumstances a million revolutions of our planet—a moment in the life of the Galaxy —may see it achieve the Inner Life. That would be good. My race would have a companion in eternity and companionship would benefit us mutually."

"You say we *may* achieve it," said David cautiously.

"Your species have certain tendencies my people never had. From your mind I can see easily that there are tendencies against the welfare of the whole."

"If you speak of such things as crime and war, then see in my mind that the vast majority of humans fights the anti-social tendencies and that though our progress against them is slow, it is certain."

"I see that. I see more. I see that you yourself are eager for the welfare of the whole. You have a strong and healthy mind, the essence of which I would not be sorry to see made into one of ours. I would like to help you in your strivings."

"How?" demanded David.

"Your mind is full of suspicion again. Relieve your tension. My help would not be through personal interference in the activities of your people, I assure you. Such interference would be incomprehensible to yourselves and undignified for myself. Let me suggest instead the two inadequacies which you are most aware of in yourself.

"First, since you are composed of unstable ingredients, you are a creature of no permanence. Not only will you decompose and dissolve in a few revolutions of the planet, but if before then you are subjected to any of a thousand different stresses, you will die. Secondly, you feel that you can work best in secrecy, yet not long ago a fellow creature recognized your true identity although you had pretended to a different identity altogether. Is what I have said true?"

David said, "It is true. But what can you do about it?"

The deep voice said, "It is already done and in your hand."

And there was a soft-textured something in David Starr's hand. His fingers almost let it drop before they realized they were holding it. It was a nearly weightless strip of—— Well, of what?

The deep voice answered the unspoken thought placidly. "It is neither gauze, nor fiber, nor plastic, nor metal. It is not matter at all as your mind understands matter. It is ———. Put it over your eyes."

David did as he was told, and it sprang from his hands

as though it had a primitive life of its own, folding softly and warmly against every fold of structure of his forehead, eyes, and nose; yet it did not prevent him from breathing or from blinking his eyes.

"What has been accomplished?" he asked.

Before the words were out of his mouth there was a mirror before him, manufactured out of energy as silently and quickly as thought itself. In it he could see himself but dimly. His farmboy costume, from hip boots to wide lapels, appeared out of focus through a shadowy mist that changed continuously, as though it were a thin smoke that drifted yet never vanished. From his upper lip to the top of his head all was lost in a shimmer of light that blazed without blinding and through which nothing could be seen. As he stared, the mirror vanished, returning to the store of energy from which it had been momentarily withdrawn.

David asked wonderingly, "Is that how I would appear to others?"

"Yes, if those others had only the sensory equipment you yourself have."

"Yet I can see perfectly. That means that light rays enter the shield. Why may they not leave then and reveal my face?"

"They do leave, as you say, but they are changed in the passage and reveal only what you see in the mirror. To explain that properly, I must use concepts lacking in your mind's understanding."

"And the rest?" David's hands moved slowly over the smoke that encircled him. He felt nothing.

126

The deep voice again answered the voiceless thought. "*You* feel nothing. Yet what appears to you as smoke is a barrier which is resistant to short-wave radiation and impassable to material objects of larger than molecular size."

"You mean it is a personal force-shield?"

"That is a crude description, yes."

David said, "Great Galaxy, it's impossible! It has been definitely proven that no force-field small enough to protect a man from radiation and from material inertia can be generated by any machine capable of being carried by a man."

"And so it is to any science of which your fellows are capable of evolving. But the mask you wear is not a power source. It is instead a storage device of energy which, for instance, can be derived from a few moments' exposure to a sun radiating as strongly as ours is from the distance of this planet. It is, further, a mechanism for releasing that energy at mental demand. Since your own mind is incapable of controlling the power, it has been adjusted to the characteristics of your mind and will operate automatically as needed. Remove the mask now."

David lifted his hand to his eyes and, again responsive to his will, the mask fell away and was only a strip of gauze in his hand.

The deep voice spoke for a last time. "And now you must leave us, Space Ranger."

And as gently as can be imagined, consciousness left David Starr.

Nor was there any transition in his return to consciousness. It came back in its entirety. There wasn't even a moment's uncertainty as to his whereabouts; none of the "Where am I?" attitude.

He knew with surety that he was standing on his good two legs upon the surface of Mars; that he was wearing the nosepiece again and breathing through it; that behind him was the exact place at the lip of the fissure where he had thrust the rope ladder's anchor for the beginning of the descent; that to his left, half-hidden among the rocks, was the scooter which Bigman had left behind.

He even knew the exact manner in which he had been returned to the surface. It was not memory; it was information deliberately inserted in his mind, probably as a final device to impress him with the power of the Martians over matter-energy interconversions. They had dissolved a tunnel to the surface for him. They had lifted him against gravity at almost rocket speed, turning the solid rock to energy before him and congealing the energy to rock once more behind him, until he was standing on the planet's outer skin once more.

There were even words in his mind that he had never consciously heard. They were in the feminine voice of the caverns, and the words were simply these: "Have no fear, Space Ranger!"

He stepped forward and was aware that the warm, Earth-like surroundings that had been prepared for him in the cavern below no longer existed. He felt the cold the more for the contrast and the wind was stronger than any he had felt yet on Mars. The sun was low in the east as it had been when he first descended the fissure. Was that the previous dawn? He had no way of judging the passage of time during his unconscious intervals, but he felt certain his descent had not been more than two dawns before anyway.

There was a difference to the sky. It seemed bluer and the sun was redder. David frowned thoughtfully for a moment, then shrugged. He was becoming accustomed to the Martian landscape, that was all. It was beginning to seem more familiar and, through habit, he was interpreting it in the old Earthly patterns.

Meanwhile it would be better to begin the return to the farm dome immediately. The scooter was by no means so quick as a sand-car nor as comfortable. The less time spent on it the better.

He took approximate sightings among the rock formations and felt like an old hand because of it. The farmboys found their way across what seemed trackless desert by just this method. They would sight along a rock that "looked like a watermelon on a hat," proceed in that direction until level with one that "looked like a spaceship with two off-center jets" and heading between it and a farther rock that "looked like a box with its top stove in." It was a crude method but it required no instruments other than a retentive memory and a picturesque imagination, and the farmboys had those in plenty.

David was following the route Bigman had recommended for speediest return with the least chance of going wrong among the less spectacular formations. The scooter jounced along, leaping crazily when it struck ridges and kicking up the dust when it turned. David rode with it, digging his heels firmly into the sockets provided for them and holding a metal steering leash tightly in each hand. He made no effort to cut his speed. Even if the vehicle turned over, there would be little chance for much harm to himself under Martian gravity.

It was another consideration that stopped him: the queer taste in his mouth and the itch along the side of his jawbone and down the line of his backbone. There was a faint grittiness in his mouth, and he looked back with distaste at the plume of dust that jetted out behind him like rocket exhaust. Strange that it should work its way forward and around him to fill his mouth as it did.

Forward and around! *Great Galaxy!* The thought that came to him at that moment clamped a cold, stifling hand upon his heart and throat.

He slowed the scooter and headed for a rocky ridge where it could stir up no dust. There he stopped it and waited for the air to grow clear. But it didn't. His tongue worked about, tasting the inside of his mouth and shrinking from the increasing roughness that came of fine grit. He looked at the redder sun and bluer sky with new understanding. It was the general dust in the air that was scattering more light, taking the blue from the sun and adding it to the sky in general. His lips were growing dry and the itching was spreading.

There was no longer doubt about it, and with a grim intensity of purpose he flung himself upon his scooter and dashed at top speed across the rocks, gravel, and dust.

Dust!

Dust!

Even on Earth men knew intimately of the Martian dust storm, which resembled only in sound the sand-storm of the Earthly deserts. It was the deadliest storm known to the inhabited Solar System. No man, caught as David Starr was now, without a sand-car as protection, miles from the nearest shelter, had ever, in all the history of Mars, survived a dust storm. Men had rolled in death throes within fifty feet of a dome, unable to make the distance, while observers within neither dared nor could sally to the rescue without a sand-car.

David Starr knew that only minutes separated him from the same agonizing death. Already the dust was creeping remorselessly between his nosepiece and the skin of his face. He could feel it in his watering, blinking eyes.

★★★★ Chapter 12

THE MISSING PIECE

The nature of the Martian dust storm is not well understood. Like Earth's Moon, the surface of Mars is, to a large extent, covered by fine dust. Unlike the Moon, Mars possesses an atmosphere capable of stirring up that dust. Usually this is not a serious matter. The Martian atmosphere is thin and winds are not long-sustained.

But occasionally, for reasons unknown, though possibly connected with electron bombardments from space, the dust becomes electrically charged and each particle repels its neighbors. Even without wind they would tend to lift upward. Each step would raise a cloud that would refuse to settle, but would drift and wisp out through the air.

When to this a wind is added, a fully developed dust storm might be said to exist. The dust is never thick enough to obscure vision; that isn't its danger. It is rather the pervasiveness of the dust that kills.

The dust particles are extremely fine and penetrate everywhere. Clothes cannot keep them out; the shelter of a rocky ledge means nothing; even the nosepiece with its broad gasket fitting against the face is helpless to prevent the individual particle from working its way through.

At the height of a storm two minutes would suffice to arouse an unbearable itching, five minutes would virtually blind a man, and fifteen minutes would kill him. Even a mild storm, so gentle that it may not even be noticed by the people exposed, is sufficient to redden exposed skin in what are called dust burns.

David Starr knew all this and more. He knew that his own skin was reddening. He was coughing without its having any effect on clearing his caking throat. He had tried clamping his mouth shut, blowing his breath out during exhalations through the smallest opening he could manage. It didn't help. The dust crept in, working its way past his lips. The scooter was jerking irregularly now as the dust did to its motor what it was doing to David.

His eyes were swollen nearly closed now. The tears that streamed out were accumulating against the gasket at the bottom of the nosepiece and were fogging the eyepieces, through which he could see nothing anyway.

Nothing could stop those tiny dust particles but the elaborately machined seams of a dome or a sand-car. Nothing.

Nothing?

Through the maddening itch and the racking cough he was thinking desperately of the Martians. Would they have known that a dust storm was brewing? *Could* they have? Would they have sent him to the surface if they had known? From his mind they must have gleaned the information that he had only a scooter to carry him back to the dome. They might have as easily transported him to the surface just outside the farm dome, or, for that matter, even inside the dome.

They *must* have known conditions were right for a dust storm. He remembered how the being with the deep voice had been so abrupt in his decision to return David to the surface, as though he hurried in order that time might be allowed for David to be caught in the storm.

And yet the last words of the feminine voice, the words he had not consciously heard and which, therefore, he was certain had been inserted in his mind while he was being borne through rock to the surface, were: "Have no fear, Space Ranger."

Even as he thought all this he knew the answer. One hand was fumbling in his pocket, the other at his nosepiece. As the nosepiece lifted off, the partially protected nose and eyes received a fresh surge of dust, burning and irritating.

He had the irresistible desire to sneeze, but fought it back. The involuntary intake of breath would fill his lungs with quantities of the dust. That in itself might be fatal.

But he was bringing up the strip of gauze he had taken

from his pocket, letting it wrap about his eyes and nose, and then over it he slapped the nosepiece again.

Only then did he sneeze. It meant he drew in vast quantities of Mars's useless atmospheric gases, but no dust was coming. He followed that by force-breathing, gasping in as much oxygen as he could and puffing it out, flinging the dust of his mouth away; alternating that with deliberate inhalations through the mouth to prevent any oncoming of oxygen drunkenness.

Gradually, as the tears washed the dust out of his eyes and no new dust entered, he found he could see again. His limbs and body were obscured by the smokiness of the force-shield that surrounded him, and he knew the upper part of his head to be invisible in the glow of his mask.

Air molecules could penetrate the shield freely, but, small though they were, the dust particles were large enough to be stopped. David could see the process with the naked eye. As each dust particle struck the shield, it was halted and the energy of its motion converted into light, so that at its point of attempted penetration a tiny sparkle showed. David found his body an ocean of such sparkles crowding one another, all the brighter as the Martian sun, red and smokily dim through the dust, allowed the ground below to remain in semi-darkness.

David slapped and brushed at his clothing. Dust clouds arose, too fine to see even if the cloudiness of the shield had not prevented sight in any case. The dust left but could not return. Gradually he became almost clear of the particles. He looked dubiously at the scooter and at-

---

tempted to start its motor. He was rewarded only by a short, grating noise and then silence. It was to be expected. Unlike the sand-cars, scooters did not, *could* not, have enclosed motors.

He would have to walk. The thought was not a particularly frightening one. The farm dome was little more than two miles away and he had plenty of oxygen. His cylinders were full. The Martians had seen to that before sending him back.

He thought he understood them now. They *did* know the dust storm was coming. They might even have helped it along. It would be strange if, with their long experience with Martian weather and their advanced science, they had not learned the fundamental causes and mechanisms of dust storms. But in sending him out to face the storm, they knew he had the perfect defense in his pocket. They had not warned him of either the ordeal that awaited him or of the defense he carried. It made sense. If he were the man who deserved the gift of the force-shield, he would, or should, think of it himself. If he did not, he was the wrong man for the job.

David smiled grimly even as he winced at the touch of his clothing against inflamed skin as he stretched his legs across the Martian terrain. The Martians were coldly unemotional in risking his life, but he could almost sympathize with them. He had thought quickly enough to save himself, but he denied himself any pride in that. He should have thought of the mask much sooner.

The force-shield that surrounded him was making it

easier to travel. He noted that the shield covered the soles of his boots so that they never made contact with the Martian surface but came to rest some quarter inch above it. The repulsion between himself and the planet was an elastic one, as though he were on many steel springs. That, combined with the low gravity, enabled him to devour the distance between himself and the dome in swinging giant strides.

He was in a hurry. More than anything else at the moment he felt the need of a hot bath.

By the time David reached one of the outer locks of the farm dome the worst of the storm was over and the light flashes on his force-shield had thinned to occasional sparks. It was safe to remove the mask from his eyes.

When the locks had opened for him, there were first of all stares, and then cries, as the farmboys on duty swarmed about him.

"Jumping Jupiter, it's Williams!"

"Where've you been, boy?"

"What happened?"

And above the confused cries and simultaneous questioning there came the shrill cry, "How did you get through the dust storm?"

The question penetrated, and there was a short silence. Someone said, "Look at his face. It's like a peeled tomato."

That was an exaggeration, but there was enough truth to it to impress all who were there. Hands were yanking at his collar which had been tightly bound about his neck in the fight against the Martian cold. They shuffled him into a seat and put in a call for Hennes.

Hennes arrived in ten minutes, hopping off a scooter and approaching with a look that was compounded of annoyance and anger. There were no visible signs of any relief at the safe return of a man in his employ.

He barked, "What's this all about, Williams?"

David lifted his eyes and said coolly, "I was lost."

"Oh, is that what you call it? Gone for two days and you were just lost. How did you manage it?"

"I thought I'd take a walk and I walked too far."

"You thought you needed a breath of air, so you've been walking through two Martian nights? Do you expect me to believe that?"

"Are any sand-cars missing?"

One of the farmboys interposed hastily as Hennes reddened further. "He's knocked out, Mr. Hennes. He was out in the dust storm."

Hennes said, "Don't be a fool. If he were out in the dust storm, he wouldn't be sitting here alive."

"Well, I know," the farmboy said, "but look at him."

Hennes looked at him. The redness of his exposed neck and shoulders was a fact that could not be easily argued away.

He said, "Were you in the storm?"

"I'm afraid so," said David.

"How did you get through?"

"There was a man," said David. "A man in smoke and light. The dust didn't bother him. He called himself the Space Ranger."

The men were gathering close. Hennes turned on them furiously, his plump face working.

"Get the Space out of here!" he yelled. "Back to your work. And you, Jonnitel, get a sand-car out here."

It was nearly an hour before the hot bath he craved was allowed David. Hennes permitted no one else to approach him. Over and over again, as he paced the floor of his private office, he would stop in midstride, whirl in sudden fury, and demand of David, "What about this Space Ranger? Where did you meet him? What did he say? What did he do? What's this smoke and light you speak of?"

To all of which David would only shake his head slightly and say, "I took a walk. I got lost. A man calling himself the Space Ranger brought me back."

Hennes gave up eventually. The dome doctor took charge. David got his hot bath. His body was anointed with creams and injected with the proper hormones. He could not avoid the injection of Soporite as well. He was asleep almost before the needle was withdrawn.

He woke to find himself between clean, cool sheets in the sick bay. The reddening of the skin had subsided considerably. They would be at him again, he knew, but he would have to fight them off but a little while longer.

He was sure he had the answer to the food-poisoning mystery now; almost the whole answer. He needed only a missing piece or two, and, of course, legal proof.

He heard the light footstep beyond the head of his bed and stiffened slightly. Was it going to begin again so soon? But it was only Benson who moved into his line of vision. Benson, with his plump lips pursed, his thin hair in disarray, his whole face a picture of worry. He carried something that looked like an old-fashioned clumsy gun.

He said, "Williams, are you awake?"

David said, "You see I am."

Benson passed the back of his hand across a perspiring forehead. "They don't know I'm here. I shouldn't be, I suppose."

"Why not?"

"Hennes is convinced you're involved with this food poisoning. He's been raving to Makian and myself about it. He claims you've been out somewhere and have nothing to say about it now other than ridiculous stories. Despite anything I can do, I'm afraid you're in terrible trouble."

"Despite anything you can do? You don't believe Hennes' theory about my complicity in all this?"

Benson leaned forward, and David could feel his breath warm on his face as he whispered, "No, I don't. I don't because I think your story is true. That's why I've come here. I must ask you about this creature you speak of, the one you claim was covered with smoke and light. Are you sure it wasn't a hallucination, Williams?"

"I saw him," said David.

"How do you know he was human? Did he speak English?"

"He didn't speak, but he was shaped like a human." David's eyes fastened upon Benson. "Do you think it was a Martian?"

"Ah"—Benson's lips drew back in a spasmodic smile— "you remember my theory. Yes, I think it was a Martian. Think, man, *think!* They're coming out in the open now and every piece of information may be vital. We have so little time."

"Why so little time?" David raised himself to one elbow.

"Of course you don't know what's happened since you've been gone, but frankly, Williams, we are all of us in despair now." He held up the gun-like affair in his hand and said bitterly, "Do you know what this is?"

"I've seen you with it before."

"It's my sampling harpoon; it's my own invention. I take it with me when I'm at the storage bins in the city. It shoots a little hollow pellet attached to it by a metal-mesh cord into a bin of, let us say, grain. At a certain time after shooting an opening appears in the front of the pellet long enough to allow the hollow within to become packed with grain. After that the pellet closes again. I drag it back and empty out the random sample it has accumulated. By varying the time after shooting in which the pellet opens, samples can be taken at various depths in the bin."

David said, "That's ingenious, but why are you carrying it now?"

"Because I'm wondering if I oughtn't to throw it into the disposal unit after I leave you. It was my only weapon for fighting the poisoners. It has done me no good so far, and can certainly do me no good in the future."

"What has happened?" David seized the other's shoulder and gripped it hard. "Tell me."

Benson winced at the pain. He said, "Every member of the farming syndicates has received a new letter from whoever is behind the poisoning. There's no doubt that the letters and the poisonings are caused by the same men, or, rather, entities. The letters admit it now."

"What do they say?"

Benson shrugged. "What difference do the details make? What it amounts to is a demand for complete surrender on our part or the food-poisoning attacks will be multiplied a thousandfold. I believe it can and will be done, and if that happens, Earth and Mars, the whole system, in fact, will panic."

He rose to his feet. "I've told Makian and Hennes that I believe you, that your Space Ranger is the clue to the whole thing, but they won't believe me. Hennes, I think, even suspects that I'm in it with you."

He seemed absorbed in his own wrongs.

David said, "How long do we have, Benson?"

"Two days. No, that was yesterday. We have thirty-six hours now."

Thirty-six hours!

David would have to work quickly. Very quickly. But maybe there would yet be time. Without knowing it Benson had given him the missing piece to the mystery.

★ ★ ★ ★ Chapter 13

THE COUNCIL TAKES OVER

Benson left some ten minutes later. Nothing that David told him satisfied him with regard to his theories connecting Martians and poisoning, and his uneasiness grew rapidly.

He said, "I don't want Hennes catching me. We've had—words."

"What about Makian? He's on our side, isn't he?"

"I don't know. He stands to be ruined by day after tomorrow. I don't think he has enough spine left to stand up to the fellow. Look, I'd better go. If you think of anything, anything at all, get it to me somehow, will you?"

He held out a hand. David took it briefly, and then Benson was gone.

David sat up in bed. His own uneasiness had grown since he had awakened. His clothes were thrown over a chair at the other end of the room. His boots stood up-right by the side of the bed. He had not dared inspect them in Benson's presence; had scarcely dared look at them.

Perhaps, he thought pessimistically, they had not tampered with them. A farmboy's hip boots are inviolate. Stealing from a farmboy's hip boots, next to stealing his sand-car in the open desert, was the unforgivable crime. Even in death, a farmboy's boots were buried with him, with the contents unremoved.

David groped inside the inner pocket of each boot in turn, and his fingers met nothingness. There had been a handkerchief in one, a few odd coins in the other. Undoubtedly they had gone through his clothing; he had expected that. But apparently they had not drawn the line at his boots. He held his breath as his arm dived into the recesses of one boot. The soft leather reached to his armpit and crumpled down as his fingers stretched out to the toes. A surge of pure gladness filled him as he felt the soft gauze-like material of the Martian mask.

He had hidden it there on general principles before the bath, but he had not anticipated the Soporite. It was luck, purely, that they had not searched the toes of his boots. He would have to be more careful henceforward.

He put the mask into a boot pocket and clipped it shut. He picked up the boots; they had been polished while he slept, which was good of someone, and showed the almost instinctive respect which the farmboy had for boots, anyone's boots.

His clothes had been put through the Refresher Spray as well. The shining plastic fibers of which they were composed had a brand-new smell about them. The pockets were all empty, of course, but underneath the chair all the contents were in a careless heap. He sorted them out. Nothing seemed to be missing. Even the handkerchief and coins from his boot pockets were there.

He put on underclothes and socks, the one-piece overall, and then the boots. He was buckling his belt when a brown-bearded farmboy stepped in.

David looked up. He said coldly, "What do you want, Zukis?"

The farmboy said, "Where do you think you're going, Earthie?" His little eyes were glaring viciously, and to David the other's expression was much the same as it had been the first day he had laid eyes on him. David could recall Hennes's sand-car outside the Farm Employment Office, himself just settling into the seat, and the bearded angry face glowering at him, while a weapon fired before he could move to defend himself.

"Nowhere," said David, "that I need ask your permission."

"That so? You're wrong, mister, because you're staying right here. Hennes' orders." Zukis blocked the door with his body. Two blasters were conspicuously displayed at either side of his drooping belt.

Zukis waited. Then, his greasy beard splitting in two as he smiled yellowly, he said, "Think maybe you've changed your mind, Earthie?"

"Maybe," said David. He added, "Someone got in to

145

see me just now. How come? Weren't you watching?"

"Shut up," snarled Zukis.

"Or were you paid off to look the other way for a while? Hennes might not like that."

Zukis spat, missing David's boots by half an inch.

David said, "You want to toss out your blasters and try that again?"

Zukis said, "Just watch out if you want any feeding, Earthie."

He closed and locked the door behind him as he left. A few minutes passed and there was the sound of clattering metal against it as it opened again. Zukis carried a tray. There was the yellow of squash on it and the green of something leafy.

"Vegetable salad," said Zukis. "Good enough for you."

A blackened thumb showed over one end of the tray. The other end balanced upon the back of his wrist so that the farmboy's hand was not visible.

David straightened, leaping to one side, bending his legs under him and bringing them down upon the mattress of the bed. Zukis, caught by surprise, turned in alarm, but David, using the springs of the mattress as extra leverage, launched into the air.

He collided heavily with the farmboy, brought down one hand flatly on the tray, ripping it out of the other's grasp and hurling it to the ground while twining his other hand in the farmboy's beard.

Zukis dropped, yelling hoarsely. David's booted foot came down on the farmboy's hand, the one that had been hidden under the tray. The other's yell became an agonized scream as the smashed fingers flew open, releasing the cocked blaster they had been holding.

David's hand whipped away from the beard and caught the other's unharmed wrist as it groped for the second blaster. He brought it up roughly, across the prone chest, under the head and out again. He pulled.

"Quiet," he said, "or I'll tear your arm loose from its socket."

Zukis subsided, his eyes rolling, his breath puffing out wetly. He said, "What are you after?"

"Why were you hiding the blaster under the tray?"

"I had to protect myself, didn't I? In case you jumped me while my hands were full of tray?"

"Then why didn't you send someone else with the tray and cover him?"

"I didn't think of that," whined Zukis.

David tightened pressure a bit and Zukis's mouth twisted in agony. "Suppose you tell the truth, Zukis."

"I—I was going to kill you."

"And what would you have told Makian?"

"You were—trying to escape."

"Was that your own idea?"

"No. It was Hennes'. Get Hennes. I'm just following orders."

David released him. He picked up one blaster and flicked the other out of its holster. "Get up."

Zukis rolled over on one side. He groaned as he tried to lift his weight on a mashed right hand and nearly torn left shoulder.

"What are you going to do? You wouldn't shoot an unarmed man, would you?"

"Wouldn't you?" asked David.

A new voice broke in. "Drop those guns, Williams," it said crisply.

David moved his head quickly. Hennes was in the doorway, blaster leveled. Behind him was Makian, face gray and etched with lines. Hennes's eyes showed his intentions plainly enough and his blaster was ready.

David dropped the blasters he had just torn from Zukis.

"Kick them over," said Hennes.

David did so.

"Now. What happened?"

David said, "You know what happened. Zukis tried a little assassination at your orders and I didn't sit still and take it."

Zukis was gabbling. "No, sir, Mr. Hennes. No, sir. It was no such thing. I was bringing in his lunch when he jumped me. My hands were full of tray; I had no chance to defend myself."

"Shut up," said Hennes contemptuously. "We'll have a talk about that later. Get out of here and be back with a couple of pinions in less than no time."

Zukis scrambled out.

Makian said mildly, "Why the pinions, Hennes?"

"Because this man is a dangerous impostor, Mr. Makian. You remember I brought him in because he seemed to know something about the food poisoning."

"Yes. Yes, of course."

148

"He told us a story about a younger sister being poisoned by Martian jam, remember? I checked on that. There haven't been too many deaths by poisoning that have reached the authorities the way this man claimed his sister's death had. Less than two hundred and fifty, in fact. It was easy to check them all and I had that done. None on record involved a twelve-year-old girl, with a brother of Williams' age, who died over a jar of jam."

Makian was startled. "How long have you known this, Hennes?"

"Almost since he came here. But I let it go. I wanted to see what he was after. I set Griswold to watching him——"

"To trying to kill me, you mean," interrupted David.

"Yes, you would say that, considering that you killed him because he was fool enough to let you suspect him." He turned back to Makian. "Then he managed to wiggle himself in with that soft-headed sap, Benson, where he could keep close check on our progress in investigating the poisoning. Then, as the last straw, he slipped out of the dome three nights ago for a reason he won't explain. You want to know why? He was reporting to the men who hired him—the ones who are behind all this. It's more than just a coincidence that the ultimatum came while he was gone."

"And where were you?" demanded David suddenly. "Did you stop keeping tabs on me after Griswold died? If you knew I was gone on the kind of deal you suspected, why wasn't a party sent out after me?"

Makian looked puzzled, and began, "Well——"

But David interrupted. "Let me finish, Mr. Makian. I think that maybe Hennes wasn't in the dome the night I left and even the day and night after I left. Where were you, Hennes?"

Hennes stepped forward, his mouth twisting. David's cupped hand was near his face. He did not believe Hennes would shoot, but he was ready to use the shield-mask if he had to.

Makian placed a nervous hand on Hennes's shoulder. "I suggest we leave him for the Council."

David said quickly, "What is this about the Council?"

"None of your business," snarled Hennes.

Zukis was back with the pinions. They were flexible plastic rods that could be bent in any way and then frozen in position. They were infinitely stronger than ropes or even metal handcuffs.

"Hold out your hands," ordered Hennes.

David did so without a word. The pinion was wrapped twice about his wrists. Zukis, leering, drew them savagely tight then drew out the pin, which action resulted in an automatic molecular rearrangement that hardened the plastic. The energy developed in that re-arrangement made the plastic warm to the touch. Another pinion went about David's ankles.

David sat quietly down upon the bed. In one hand he still had the shield-mask. Makian's remark about the Council was proof enough to David that he would not remain pinioned long. Meanwhile he was content to allow matters to develop further.

He said again, "What's this about the Council?"

But he need not have asked. There was a yell from outside, and a catapulting figure hurled itself through the door with the cry of, "Where's Williams?"

It was Bigman himself, as large as life, which wasn't very large. He was paying no attention to anything but David's seated figure. He was speaking rapidly and breathlessly. "I didn't hear you were through a dust storm till I landed inside the dome. Sizzling Ceres, you must have been fried. How did you get through it? I— I—"

He noticed David's position for the first time, and turned furiously. "Who in Space has the boy tied up like this?"

Hennes had caught his breath by now. One of his hands shot out and caught Bigman's overall collar in a brutal grip that lifted his slight body off the floor. "I told you what would happen, slug, if I caught you here again."

Bigman yelled, "Let go, you pulp-mouth jerk! I've got a right in here. I give you a second and a half to let me go or you'll answer to the Council of Science."

Makian said, "For Mars' sake, Hennes, let him go."

Hennes let him drop. "Get out of here."

"Not on your life. I'm an accredited employee of the Council. I came here with Dr. Silvers. Ask him."

He nodded at the tall, thin man just outside the door. His name suited him. His hair was silver-white and he had a mustache of the same shade.

"If you'll pardon me," said Dr. Silvers, "I would like to take charge of matters. The government at International City on Earth has declared a state of System Emergency and all the farms will be under the control of the Council of Science henceforward. I have been assigned to take over the Makian Farms."

"I expected something like this," muttered Makian unhappily.

"Remove this man's pinions," ordered Dr. Silvers.

Hennes said, "He's dangerous."

"I will take full responsibility."

Bigman jumped and clicked his heels. "On your way, Hennes."

Hennes paled in anger, but no words came.

Three hours had passed when Dr. Silvers met Makian and Hennes again in Makian's private quarters.

He said, "I'll want to go over all the production records of this farm for the last six months. I will have to see your Dr. Benson with regard to whatever advances he has made in connection with solving this food-poisoning problem. We have six weeks to break this matter. No more."

"Six weeks," exploded Hennes. "You mean one day."

"No, sir. If we haven't the answer by the time the ultimatum expires, all exports of food from Mars will be stopped. We will not give in while a single chance remains."

"By Space," said Hennes. "Earth will starve."

"Not for six weeks," said Dr. Silvers. "Food supplies will last that long, with rationing."

"There'll be panic and rioting," said Hennes.

"True," said Dr. Silvers grimly. "It will be most un-pleasant."

"You'll ruin the farm syndicates," groaned Makian.

"It will be ruined anyway. Now, I intend to see Dr. Benson this evening. We will have a four-way confer-ence tomorrow at noon. Tomorrow midnight, if noth-ing breaks anywhere on Mars or at the Moon's Central Laboratories, the embargo goes into effect and arrange-ments will be made for an all-Mars conference of the various syndicate members."

"Why?" asked Hennes.

"Because," said Dr. Silvers, "there is reason to think that whoever is behind this mad crime must be con-nected with the farms closely. They know too much about the farms for any other conclusion to be arrived at."

"What about Williams?"

"I've questioned him. He sticks to his story, which is, I'll admit, queer enough. I've sent him to the city, where he'll be questioned further; under hypnosis, if neces-sary."

The door signal flashed.

Dr. Silvers said, "Open the door, Mr. Makian."

Makian did so, as though he were not owner of one of the largest farms on Mars and, by virtue of that fact, one of the richest and most powerful men in the Solar Sys-tem.

Bigman stepped in. He looked at Hennes challengingly. He said, "Williams is on a sand-car heading back for the city under guard."

"Good," said Dr. Silvers, his thin lips set tightly.

A mile outside the farm dome the sand-car stopped. David Starr, nosepiece in place, stepped out. He waved to the driver, who leaned out and said, "Remember! Lock 7! We'll have one of our men there to let you in."

David smiled and nodded. He watched the sand-car continue its trip toward the city and then turned back on foot to the farm dome.

The men of the Council co-operated, of course. They had helped him in his desire to leave openly and to return secretly, but none of them, not even Dr. Silvers, knew the purpose of his request.

He had the pieces to the puzzle, but he still needed the proof.

★ ★ ★ ★ Chapter 14

"I AM THE SPACE RANGER!"

Hennes entered his bedroom in a haze compounded equally of weariness and anger. The weariness was simple. It was nearing 3 A.M. He had not had too much rest the last two nights or, for that matter, much relief of tension in the last six months. Yet he had felt it necessary to sit through the session this Dr. Silvers of the Council had had with Benson.

Dr. Silvers had not liked that, and that accounted for one bit of the anger that drenched and drowned him. Dr. Silvers! An old incompetent who came bustling down from the city thinking he could get to the bottom of the trouble in a day and a night when all the science of Earth and Mars had been exerting itself for months to no avail. And Hennes was angry at Makian as well for becoming as limp as well-oiled boots and nothing more than the simple lackey of the white-headed fool. Makian!

Two decades ago he had been almost a legend as the toughest owner of the toughest farm on Mars.

There was Benson, too, and his interference with Hennes' plans for settling the interfering greenhorn, this Williams, in the quickest and easiest way. And Griswold and Zukis, who were too stupid to carry through the necessary steps that would have won over the weakness of Makian and the sentimentality of Benson.

He pondered briefly the advisability of a Soporite pill. On this night he wanted rest for the necessary keenness of the next day and yet his anger might keep sleep away.

He shook his head. No. He could not risk drugged helplessness in the event of some crucial turn of events in the night.

He compromised by throwing the toggle switch that magnetically bound the door in place. He even tested the door briefly to make sure the electromagnetic circuits worked. Personal doors, in the totally masculine and informal life of a farm dome, were so infrequently locked that it was not uncommon to have insulation wear through, wires fall loose, without anyone being the wiser over the years. His own door had not been locked, to his knowledge, since he had first taken the job.

The circuit was in order. The door did not even tremble as he pulled at it. So much for that.

He sighed heavily, sat down upon the bed, and removed his boots, first one, then the other. He rubbed his feet wearily, sighed again, then stiffened; stiffened so suddenly that he shot off the bed without really being aware of moving.

His stare was one of complete bewilderment. It couldn't be. *It couldn't be!* It would mean that Williams's foolish story was true. It would mean that Benson's ridiculous mouthings about Martians might, after all, turn out to be——

No, he refused to believe that. It would be easier to believe that his lack-sleep mind was having a private joke.

Yet the dark of the room was alight with the cold blue-white brilliance that carried no glare with it. By it he could see the bed, the walls, the chair, the dresser, even his boots, standing where he had just placed them. And he could see the man creature with only a blaze of light where a head ought to be and no distinct feature elsewhere; rather a kind of smoke instead.

He felt the wall against his back. He had not been conscious of his retreat backward.

The object spoke, and the words were hollow and booming as though they carried an echo with them.

The object said, "I am the Space Ranger!"

Hennes drew himself up. First surprise over, he forced himself into calmness. In a steady voice he said, "What do you want?"

The Space Ranger did not move or speak, and Hennes found his eyes fastened upon the apparition.

The foreman waited, his chest pumping, and still the thing of smoke and light did not move. It might have been a robot geared to make the one statement of identity. For a moment Hennes wondered if that might be the case, and surrendered the thought as soon as it was born. He was standing next to the chest of drawers, and not all his wonder allowed him to forget that fact. Slowly his hand was moving.

In the light of the thing itself his motion was not invisible, but it paid no attention. Hennes's hand was resting lightly on the surface of the bureau in a pretense of innocent gesture. The robot, Martian, man, whatever it was, Hennes thought, would not know the secret of that bureau. It had hidden in the room, waiting, but it had not searched the room. Or if it had done so, it had been a most skillful job, since even now Hennes's flicking eye could note no single abnormal thing about the room; nothing misplaced; nothing where it should not be, except for the Space Ranger itself.

His fingers touched a little notch in the wood. It was a common mechanism and few farm managers on Mars lacked one. In a way it was old-fashioned, as old-fashioned as the imported wooden bureau itself, a tradition dating back to the lawless old days of the farming pioneers, but tradition dies hard. The little notch moved slightly under his fingernail and a panel in the side of the chest dropped outward. Hennes was ready for it, and his hand was a blur of motion toward the blaster which the moving panel had revealed.

He held the blaster now, aimed dead center, and in all that time the creature had not moved. What passed for arms dangled emptily.

Hennes found confidence sweeping back. Robot, Martian, or man, the object could not withstand a blaster. It was a small weapon, and the projectile it hurled was almost contemptible in size. The old-fashioned "guns" of ancient days carried metal slugs that were rocks in comparison. But the small projectile of the blaster was far more deadly. Once set in motion, anything that stopped it tripped a tiny atomic trigger that converted a sub-microscopic fraction of its mass into energy, and in that conversion the object that stopped it, whether rock, metal, or human flesh, was consumed to the accompaniment of a tiny noise like the flick of a fingernail against rubber.

Hennes said in a tone that borrowed menace from the blaster he held, "Who are you? What do you want?"

Once again the object spoke, and once again it said slowly, "I am the Space Ranger!"

Hennes's lips curved in cold ferocity as he fired.

The projectile left the muzzle, raced squarely at the object of smoke, reached it, and stopped. It stopped instantaneously, without touching the body that was still one quarter of an inch beyond its final penetration. Even the concussion of collision was not carried beyond the force-shield barrier which absorbed all the projectile's momentum, converting it into a flare of light.

That flare of light was never seen. It was drowned out in the intense blaze that was the blaster projectile exploding into energy as it stopped with no surrounding matter to shield the blast of light. It was as though a pin-sized sun existed in the room for a tiny fraction of a second.

Hennes, with a wild yell, threw his hands to his eyes as though to protect them against a physical blow. It was too late. Minutes later, when he dared open his eyelids, his aching, burning eyes could tell him nothing. Open or closed, he saw only red-studded blackness. He could not see the Space Ranger whirl into motion, pounce upon his boots, search their pockets with flying fingers, break the door's magnetic circuit, and slip out of the room seconds before the inevitable crowd of people with their confused cries of alarm had begun to gather.

Hennes's hand still covered his eyes when he heard them. He called, "Get the thing! Get him! He's in the room. Tackle him, you Mars-forsaken, black-booted cowards."

"There's no one in the room," half-a-dozen voices called, and someone added, "Smells like a blaster, though."

A firmer, more authoritative voice said, "What's wrong, Hennes?" It was Dr. Silvers.

"Intruders," said Hennes, shaking in frustration and wrath. "Doesn't anyone see him? What's the matter with all of you? Are you——" He couldn't say the word. His blinking eyes were watering and blurred light was just beginning to make its way into them again. He couldn't say "blind."

Silvers asked, "Who was the intruder? Can you describe him?"

And Hennes could only shake his head helplessly. How could he explain? Could he tell them of a nightmare of smoke that could speak and against which a blaster bullet could only explode prematurely and without damage except to the man who sped it on its way?

Dr. James Silvers made his way back to his room in dull gloom. This disturbance that had routed him out of his room before he had completed preparation for bed, this aimless running about of men, the tongue-tied lack of explanation on the part of Hennes, all were to him nothing but a series of pinpricks. His eyes were fixed on tomorrow.

He had no faith in victory, no faith in the efficacy of any embargo. Let the food shipments stop. Let even a few on Earth find out why, or, worse still, invent their own theories therefor, and the results might be more frightful than any mass poisoning.

This young David Starr expressed confidence, but so far his actions inspired none in himself. His story of a Space Ranger was a poorly calculated one, fit only to arouse the suspicions of men such as Hennes and bringing him almost to his death. It was fortunate for the youngster that he, Silvers, had arrived at the proper time. Nor had he explained the reasons for such a story. He had merely expounded his plans for leaving the city and then secretly returning. Yet when Silvers had first received Starr's letter, brought by the little fellow, the one that called himself Bigman in tremendous defiance of the truth, he had quickly checked with Council headquarters on Earth. It had confirmed that David Starr was to be obeyed in all particulars.

Yet how could such a young man——

Dr. Silvers halted. That was strange! The door to his room, which he had left ajar in his haste, was still ajar, but no light shone out into the hall. Yet he had not put it out before leaving. He could remember its glow behind him as he had hastened down the hall toward the stairs.

Had someone put it out for him on some strange impulse toward economy? It seemed hardly likely.

There was no sound within the room. He drew his blaster, threw the door open, and stepped firmly to where he knew the light switch to be located.

A hand dropped over his mouth.

He squirmed, but the arm was a large and muscular one, and the voice in his ear was familiar.

"It's all right, Dr. Silvers. I just didn't want you to give me away by yelling in surprise."

The arm dropped away. Dr. Silvers said, "Starr?"

"Yes. Close the door. It seemed your room would be the best hiding place while the search goes on. In any case, I must speak to you. Did Hennes say what had happened?"

"No, not really. Were you involved in that?"

David's smile was lost in the darkness. "In a way, Dr. Silvers. Hennes was visited by the Space Ranger, and in the confusion I was able to reach your room with no one, I hope, having seen me."

The old scientist's voice rose despite himself. "What are you saying? I am in no mood for jokes."

"I am not joking. The Space Ranger exists."

"That will not do. The story did not impress Hennes and I deserve the truth."

"It impresses Hennes now, I am sure, and you will have the truth when tomorrow is done. Meanwhile, listen to me. The Space Ranger, as I say, exists, and he is our great hope. The game we play is a rickety one and though I know who is behind the poisoning, the knowledge may be useless. It is not a criminal or two, intending to gain a few millions by colossal blackmail, that we face, but rather a well-organized group that intends to gain control of the entire Solar System. It can carry on, I am convinced, even if we pick off the leaders, unless we learn enough of the details of the conspiracy to stop its workings cold."

"Show me the leader," said Dr. Silvers grimly, "and the Council will learn all necessary details."

"Never quickly enough," said David, just as grimly. "We must have the answer, *all* the answer, in less than twenty-four hours. Victory after that will not stop the death of millions upon Earth."

Dr. Silvers said, "What do you plan then?"

"In theory," said David, "I know who the poisoner is and how the poisoning was accomplished. To be met with anything but a flat denial on the part of the poisoner I need a bit of material proof. That I will have before the evening is over. To gain from him, even then, the necessary information, we must break his morale completely. There we must use the Space Ranger. Indeed, he has begun the process of morale-cracking already."

"The Space Ranger again. You are bewitched by this thing. If he does exist, if this is not a trick of yours in which even I must be a victim, who is he and what is he? How do you know he is not deceiving you?"

"I can tell no one the details of that. I can only tell

you that I know him to be on the side of humanity. I
trust him as I would myself, and I will take full responsibility for him. You must do as I say, Dr. Silvers, in this
matter, or I warn you we will have no choice but to
proceed without you. The importance of the game is
such that even you may not stand in my way."

There was no mistaking the firm resolution of the
voice. Dr. Silvers could not see the expression of David's
face in the darkness, but somehow he did not have to.
"What is it you wish me to do?"

"Tomorrow noon you will meet with Makian, Hennes, and Benson. Bring Bigman with you as a personal
bodyguard. He is small, but he is quick and knows no
fear. Have the Central Building protected by Council
men, and I would advise that you have them armed with
repeater blasters and gas pellets just in case. Now remember this, between twelve-fifteen and twelve-thirty leave
the rear entrance unguarded and unobserved. I will guarantee its safety. Show no surprise at whatever happens
thereafter."

"Will you be there?"

"No. My presence will not be necessary."

"Then?"

"There will be a visit from the Space Ranger. He
knows what I know, and from him the accusations will
be more shattering to the criminal."

Dr. Silvers felt hope arising in spite of himself. "Do
you think, then, that we'll succeed?"

There was a long silence. Then David Starr said,
"How can I tell? I can only hope so."

There was a longer silence. Dr. Silvers felt a tiny draft as though the door had opened. He turned to the light switch. The room flooded with light, and he found himself alone.

★ ★ ★ ★ **Chapter 15**

THE SPACE RANGER TAKES OVER

David Starr worked as quickly as he dared. Not much was left of the night. Some of the excitement and tension were beginning to fade, and the utter weariness that he had been refusing to acknowledge for hours was soaking in just a bit.

His small pencil flash flickered here and there. He hoped earnestly that what he sought for would not be behind still additional locks. If it were, he would have to use force, and he was in no mood to attract attention just then. There was no safe that he could see; nothing equivalent to such an object. That was both good and bad. What he looked for would not be out of reach, but then again it might not be in the room at all.

That would be a pity after the carefully planned manner in which he had obtained the key to this room. Hennes would not recover quickly from the working out of 'that plan.

David smiled. He himself had been almost as surprised as Hennes at the very first. His words, "I am the Space Ranger," had been the first he had spoken through the force-shield since his emergence from the Martian caverns. He could not remember what his voice had sounded like there. Perhaps he had not truly heard it. Perhaps, under Martian influence, he had simply sensed his own thoughts as he did theirs.

Here on the surface, however, the sound of his own voice had left him thunderstruck. Its hollowness and booming depth had been entirely unexpected. He recovered, of course, and understood almost immediately. Although the shield let air molecules pass, it probably slowed them. Such interference would naturally affect sound waves.

David was not exactly sorry for that. The voice, as it was, would be helpful.

The shield had worked well against the blaster radiation. The flash had not been stopped entirely; he had seen it clearly. At least the effect upon himself had been nothing compared to that upon Hennes.

Methodically, even as his weary mind turned these things over, he was inspecting the contents of shelves and cabinets.

The light beam held steady for a moment. David reached past other gadgets to pick up a small metal object. He turned it over and over in the small light. He wound a little button which set at different positions and observed what happened afterward.

His heart bounded.

It was the final proof. The proof of all his speculations —the speculations that had been so reasonable and so complete and yet had rested upon nothing more than logic. Now the logic had been borne out by something made of molecules, something that could be touched and felt.

He put it in his hip-boot pocket to join his mask and the keys he had taken from Hennes's boots earlier in the night.

He locked the door behind him and stepped out into the open. The dome above was beginning to gray visibly. Soon the main fluorescents would go on and day would officially begin. The last day, either for the poisoners or for Earth civilization as it then was.

Meanwhile there would be a chance for sleep.

The Makian farm dome lay in a frozen quiet. Few of the farmboys could even guess at what was going on. That it was something serious was, of course, obvious, but further than that it was impossible to see. Some few whispered that Makian had been caught in serious financial irregularities, but no one could believe it. It wasn't even logical, since why would they send in an army just for that?

Certainly hard-faced men in uniform circled Central Building with repeater blasters cradled in their arms. On the roof of the building two artillery pieces had been set up. And the area around it was deserted. All farmboys, except those necessary for the maintenance of essential utilities, had been restricted to barracks. Those few excepted were ordered to remain strictly at their jobs.

At 12:15 P.M. exactly, the two men patrolling the rear of the building separated, moved away, leaving that area unguarded. At twelve-thirty they returned and took up their patrols. One of the artillerymen on the roof afterward stated that he had seen someone enter the building in that interval. He admitted he had caught only a brief glimpse and his description did not make very much sense, since he said it seemed to be a man on fire.

Nobody believed him at the time.

Dr. Silvers was not certain of anything. Not at all certain. He scarcely knew how to begin the session. He looked at the other four that sat about the table.

Makian. He looked as if he hadn't slept in a week. Probably hadn't, either. He hadn't spoken a word so far. Silvers wondered if he was completely aware of his surroundings.

Hennes. He was wearing dark glasses. He took them off at one time and his eyes were bloodshot and angry. Now he sat there muttering to himself.

Benson. Quiet and unhappy. Dr. Silvers had spent several hours with him the night before and there was no doubt in his mind that the failures of his investigations were an embarrassment and a grief to him. He had spoken about Martians, native Martians, as causes of the poisonings, but Silvers had known better than to take that seriously.

Bigman. The only happy one of the lot. To be sure

he understood only a fragment of the real crisis. He was leaning back in his chair, obviously pleased at being at the same table with important people, savoring his role to the full.

And there was one additional chair that Silvers had brought to the table. It stood there, empty and waiting. No one commented on the fact.

Dr. Silvers kept the conversation going somehow, making insubstantial remarks, trying to mask his own uncertainties. Like the empty chair, he was waiting.

At twelve-sixteen he looked up and rose slowly to his feet. No words came. Bigman pushed his chair back and it went over with a crash. Hennes's head turned sharply and he grasped the table with fingers that became white with strain. Benson looked about and whimpered. Only Makian seemed unmoved. His eyes lifted, then, apparently, took in the sight merely as another incomprehensible element in a world that had grown too large and strange for him.

The figure in the doorway said, "I am the Space Ranger!"

In the bright lights of the room the glow that surrounded his head was somewhat subdued, the smoke that concealed his body somewhat more substantial than Hennes had seen it the night before.

The Space Ranger moved in. Almost automatically the seated men pushed their chairs away, clearing a place at the table, so that the one empty chair stood in lonely isolation.

The Space Ranger sat down, face invisible behind

light, smoky arms extended before him, resting on the table, and yet not resting upon it. Between the table and the arms one quarter of an inch of empty space existed.

The Space Ranger said, "I have come to speak to criminals."

It was Hennes who broke the sticky silence that followed. He said, in a voice that dripped with husky venom, "You mean burglars?"

His hand went momentarily to his dark glasses but did not remove them. His fingers shook visibly.

The Space Ranger's voice was a monotone of slow, hollow words. "It is true I am a burglar. Here are the keys I abstracted from your boots. I need them no longer."

Slivers of metal flashed across the table toward Hennes, who did not pick them up.

The Space Ranger went on, "But the burglary took place in order to prevent a greater crime. There is the crime of the trusted foreman, for instance, who periodically spent nights in Wingrad City on a one-man search for poisoners."

Bigman's little face puckered in glee. "Hey, Hennes," he called, "sounds like you're being paged."

But Hennes had eyes and ears only for the apparition across the table. He said, "What is the crime in that?"

"The crime," said the Space Ranger, "of a fast trip out in the direction of the Asteroids."

"Why? What for?"

"Is it not from the Asteroids that the poisoners' ultimata have come?"

"Are you accusing me of being behind the food poisoning? I deny it. I demand your proof. That is, if you think you need any proof. Perhaps you think that your masquerade can force me to admit a lie."

"Where were you the two nights before the final ultimatum was received?"

"I will not answer. I deny your right to question me."

"I will answer the question for you then. The machinery of the vast poisoning combine is located in the Asteroids, where what is left of the old pirate bands have gathered. The brains of the combine is here at Makian Farms."

Here Makian rose unsteadily to his feet, his mouth working.

The Space Ranger waved him down with a firm motion of his smoky arm and continued, "You, Hennes, are the go-between."

Hennes did remove his glasses now. His plump, sleek face, somewhat marred by his red-rimmed eyes, was set into a hard mold.

He said, "You bore me, Space Ranger, or whatever you call yourself. This conference, as I understand it, was for the purpose of discussing means of combating the poisoners. If it is being converted into a forum for the stupid accusations of a play actor, I am leaving."

Dr. Silvers reached across Bigman to grasp Hennes's wrist. "Please stay, Hennes. I want to hear more of this. No one will convict you without ample proof."

Hennes dashed Silvers's hand away and rose from his chair.

Bigman said quietly, "I'd love to see you shot, Hennes, which is exactly what you will be if you go out the door."

"Bigman is right," said Silvers. "There are armed men outside, with instructions to allow no one to leave without orders from me."

Hennes's fists clenched and unclenched. He said, "I will not contribute another word to this illegal procedure. You are all witnesses that I am being detained by force." He sat down again and folded his arms across his chest.

The Space Ranger began again, "And yet Hennes is only the go-between. He is too great a villain to be the real villain."

Benson said faintly, "You speak in contradictions."

"Only apparently. Consider the crime. You can learn a great deal about a criminal from the nature of the crime he commits. First, there is the fact that few people, comparatively, have died so far. Presumably the criminals could have gained what they wanted more quickly by beginning with wholesale poisonings, instead of merely threatening for six months during which they risked capture and gained nothing. What does this mean? It would seem that the leader somehow hesitates to kill. That is certainly not in character for Hennes. I have obtained most of my information from Williams, who is not among us now, and from him I know that after his arrival at the farm Hennes tried several times to arrange his murder."

Hennes forgot his resolve. He shouted, "A lie!"

The Space Ranger went on, unheeding, "So Hennes would have no compunction against killing. We would have to find someone of gentler mold. Yet what would force an essentially gentle person to kill people he has never seen, who have done him no harm? After all, though an insignificant percentage of Earth's population has been poisoned, the dead number several hundred. Fifty of them were children. Presumably, then, there is a strong drive for wealth and power which overcomes his gentleness. What lies behind that drive? A life of frustration, perhaps, which has driven him into a morbid hatred of humanity as a whole, a desire to show those who despised him how great a man he really is. We look for a man, then, who might be expected to have an advanced inferiority complex. Where can we find such a one?"

All were watching the Space Ranger now with an intentness that burned in every eye. Something of keenness had returned even to Makian's expression. Benson was frowning in thought, and Bigman had forgotten to grin.

The Space Ranger continued, "Most important as a clue is what followed the arrival of Williams at the farm. He was at once suspected of being a spy. His story of the poisoning of his sister was easily shown to be false. Hennes, as I have said, was for outright murder. The leader, with his softer conscience, would take another method.

He tried to neutralize the dangerous Williams by developing a friendship for him and pretending to unfriendliness with Hennes.

"Let us summarize. What do we know about the leader of the poisoners? He is a man with a conscience who has *seemed* friendly to Williams and unfriendly to Hennes. A man with an inferiority complex resulting from a life of frustration because he was different from others, less of a man, smaller——"

There was a rapid movement. A chair was thrust from the table, and a figure backed rapidly away, a blaster in his hand.

Benson rose to his feet and yelled, "Great Space. *Bigman!*"

Dr. Silvers cried helplessly, "But—but I was to bring him here as a bodyguard. He's armed."

For a moment Bigman stood there, blaster ready, watching each of them out of his sharp little eyes.

★ ★ ★ ★ Chapter 16

SOLUTION

Bigman said, his high voice firm, "Don't let's draw any quick conclusions now. It may sound as if the Space Ranger is describing me, but he hasn't said so yet."

They watched him. No one spoke.

Bigman flipped his blaster suddenly, caught it by the muzzle, and tossed it onto the table where it skimmed noisily across in the direction of the Space Ranger. "I say I'm not the man, and there's my weapon to show I mean it."

The Space Ranger's smoke-obscured fingers reached for it.

"I also say you're not the man," he said, and the blaster skimmed back to Bigman.

Bigman pounced upon it, shoved it back in his holster, and sat down once more. "Now suppose you keep on talking, Space Ranger."

The Space Ranger said, "It might have been Bigman,

but there are many reasons why it could not have been. In the first place, the enmity between Bigman and Hennes arose long before Williams appeared on the scene."

Dr. Silvers protested. "But look here. If the leader was pretending to be on the outs with Hennes, it might not have been just for Williams' sake. It might have been a long-standing scheme."

The Space Ranger said, "Your point is well taken, Dr. Silvers. But consider this. The leader, whoever he is, must be in complete control of the gang's tactics. He must be able to enforce his own squeamishness about killing upon a group of what are probably the most desperate outlaws in the system. There is only one way he can do that, and that is by arranging it so that they cannot possibly continue without him. How? By controlling the supply of poison and the method of poisoning. Surely Bigman could do neither."

"How do you know that?" demanded Dr. Silvers.

"Because Bigman doesn't have the training that would enable him to develop and produce a new poison more virulent than any known. He doesn't have the laboratory or the botanical and bacteriological training. He doesn't have access to the food bins at Wingrad City. All of which, however, *does apply to Benson*."

The agronomist, perspiring profusely, raised his voice in a weak yell. "What are you trying to do? Test me as you tested Bigman just now?"

"I didn't test Bigman," said the Space Ranger. "I never accused him. I do accuse you, Benson. You are the brains and leader of the food-poisoning combine."

"No. You're mad."

"Not at all. Quite sane. Williams first suspected you and passed his suspicions on to me."

"He had no reason to. I was perfectly frank with him."

"Too frank. You made the mistake of telling him that it was your opinion that Martian bacteria growing upon farm products were the source of the poison. As an agronomist, you must have known that was impossible. Martian life is not protein in nature and could no more feed on Earth plants than we could feed on rocks. So you told a deliberate lie, and that made everything else about you suspect. It made Williams wonder if perhaps you had yourself made an extract of Martian bacteria. The extract would be poisonous. Don't you think so?"

Benson cried wildly, "But how could I possibly spread the poison? You don't make sense."

"You had access to the Makian farm shipments. After the first few poisonings you could arrange to obtain samples from the storage bins at the city. You told Williams how you carefully took samples from different bins, from different levels of a single bin. You told him how you used a harpoon-like affair you invented yourself."

"But what is there wrong with that?"

"A good deal. Last night I obtained keys from Hennes. I used them to get into the one place in the farm dome which is consistently kept locked—your laboratory. There I found this." He held the small metal object up to the light.

178

Dr. Silvers said, "What is it, Space Ranger?"

"It is Benson's sample taker. It fits at the end of his food harpoon. Observe how it works."

The Space Ranger adjusted a small knob at one end. "Firing the harpoon," he said, "trips this safety catch. So! Now watch."

There was the faintest buzzing noise. It ended after five seconds, and the fore end of the sampler gaped open, remained so for a second, then closed.

"That's the way it's supposed to work," cried Benson. "I made no secret of it."

"No, you didn't," said the Space Ranger sternly. "You and Hennes had been quarreling for days over Williams. You hadn't the stomach to have him killed. At the very last you brought the harpoon with you to Williams' bedside to see if the sight of it would surprise him into some action that would give him away. It didn't, but Hennes would wait no longer, anyway. Zukis was sent in to kill him."

"But what's wrong with the sampler?" demanded Benson.

"Let me show its workings again. But this time, Dr. Silvers, please observe the side of the sampler toward yourself now."

Dr. Silvers leaned across the table, watching closely. Bigman, blaster out once more, divided his attention between Benson and Hennes. Makian was on his feet, leathery cheeks flushed.

Once again the sampler was set, once again the little mouth flew open, and this time, as they watched the

neutral side indicated, a covering sliver of metal withdrew there as well, revealing a shallow depression that
glistened gummily.

"There," said the Space Ranger, "you can see what
happened. Each time Benson took a sample, a few grains
of wheat, a piece of fruit, a leaf of lettuce was smeared
with that colorless gum, a poisonous extract of Martian
bacteria. It is a simple poison, no doubt, that is not affected by subsequent food processing and eventually
turns up in a loaf of bread, a jar of jam, a can of baby
food. It was a clever and diabolical trick."

Benson was beating on the table. "It's all a lie, a rotten
lie!"

"Bigman," said the Space Ranger, "gag the man. Stand
near him and don't let him move."

"Really," protested Dr. Silvers, "you're making a case,
Space Ranger, but you must let the man defend himself."

"There is no time," said the Space Ranger, "and proof
that will satisfy even you will be forthcoming quickly."

Bigman used his handkerchief as a gag. Benson struggled and then sat in sweating stillness as the butt of Bigman's blaster collided noisily with his skull.

"The next time," said Bigman, "it will be hard enough
to knock you out; maybe fix you up with a concussion."

The Space Ranger rose. "You all suspected, or pretended to suspect, Bigman when I spoke of a man with
an inferiority complex because he was small. There are
more ways of being small than in size. Bigman compen-
sates for his size by belligerence and loud assertion of his
own opinions. The men here respect him because of this.

Benson, however, living here on Mars among men of action finds himself despised as a 'college farmer,' ignored as a weakling, and looked down upon by men whom he considers much his inferiors. To be unable to compensate for this except by murder of the most cowardly sort is another and worse kind of smallness.

"But Benson is mentally sick. To get a confession out of him would be difficult; perhaps impossible. However, Hennes would do almost as well as a source of knowledge about the future activities of the poisoners. He could tell us exactly where in the Asteroids we could find his various henchmen. He could tell us where the supply of poison, for use at midnight tonight, is kept. He could tell us many things."

Hennes sneered. "I could tell you nothing, and I will tell you nothing. If you shoot Benson and myself right now, matters will proceed exactly as they would if we were alive. So do your worst."

"Would you talk," said the Space Ranger, "if we guaranteed your personal safety?"

"Who would believe in your guarantee?" said Hennes. "I'll stick to my story. I'm an innocent man. Killing us will do you no good."

"You realize that if you refuse to talk, millions of men, women, and children may die."

Hennes shrugged.

"Very well," said the Space Ranger. "I have been told something about the effects of the Martian poison Benson has developed. Once in the stomach, absorption is very quick; the nerves to the chest muscles are paralyzed;

the victim can't breathe. It is painful strangulation stretched over five minutes. Of course that is when the poison has been introduced into the stomach."

The Space Ranger, as he spoke, drew from his pocket a small glass pellet. He opened the sampler and drew it across the gummed surface until the glitter of the glass had been obscured by a sticky coating.

"Now if," he said, "the poison were placed just within the lips, matters would be different. It would be absorbed much more slowly and would take effect much more gradually. Makian," he called suddenly, "there's the man who betrayed you, used your farm to organize the poisoning of men and the ruin of the farm syndicates. Grab his arms and pinion them."

The Space Ranger tossed a pinion upon the table.

Makian, with a cry of long-pent range, threw himself on Hennes. For a moment wrath restored to him some of the strength of his youth and Hennes struggled in vain against him.

When Makian stepped away, Hennes was strapped to his chair, his arms drawn painfully behind and around its back, his wrists pinioned tightly.

Makian said between rasping pants, "After you talk, it will be my pleasure to take you apart with my ten fingers."

The Space Ranger circled the table now, approaching Hennes slowly, the smeared glass pellet held in two fingers before him. Hennes shrank away. At the other end of the table Benson writhed desperately, and Bigman kicked him into stillness.

The Space Ranger pinched Hennes's lower lip and drew it out, exposing his teeth. Hennes tried to snap his head away, but the Space Ranger's fingers pinched together and Hennes let out a muffled scream.

The Space Ranger dropped the pellet in the space between lip and teeth.

"I believe it will take about ten minutes before you absorb enough poison through the mouth membranes to begin taking noticeable effect," said the Space Ranger. "If you agree to talk before then, we will remove the pellet and let you rinse your mouth. Otherwise, the poison will take effect slowly. Gradually it will become more and more difficult and painful to breathe, and finally, in about an hour, you will die of very slow strangulation. And if you do die, you will have accomplished nothing, because the demonstration will be very educational for Benson and we will proceed to sweat the truth out of him."

The perspiration trickled down Hennes's temples. He made choking noises in the back of his throat.

The Space Ranger waited patiently.

Hennes cried, "I'll talk. I'll talk. Take it out! *Take it out!*"

The words were muffled through his distorted lips, but their intent and the hideous terror in every line of his face were plain enough.

"Good! You had better take notes, Dr. Silvers."

It was three days before Dr. Silvers met David Starr again. He had had little sleep in that interval and he was

183

tired, but not too tired to greet David gladly. Bigman, who had not left Silvers in all that interval, was equally effusive in his greetings.

"It worked," said Silvers. "You've heard about it, I'm sure. It worked unbelievably well."

"I know," said David, smiling. "The Space Ranger told me all about it."

"Then you've seen him since."

"Only for a moment or two."

"He disappeared almost immediately afterward. I mentioned him in my report; I had to, of course. But it certainly made me feel foolish. In any case, I have Bigman here and old Makian as witnesses."

"And myself," said David.

"Yes, of course. Well, it's over. We located the poison stores and cleaned out the Asteroids. There'll be two dozen men up for life sentences and Benson's work will actually be beneficial in the end. His experiments on Martian life were, in their way, revolutionary. It's possible a whole new series of antibiotics may be the final results of his attempts to poison Earth into submission. If the poor fool had aimed at scientific eminence, he would have ended a great man. Thank Hennes' confession for stopping him."

David said, "That confession was carefully planned for. The Space Ranger had been working on him since the night before."

"Oh, well, I doubt that any human could have withstood the danger of poisoning that Hennes was subject to. In fact, what would have happened if Hennes had been really innocent? The chance the Space Ranger took was a big one."

"Not really. There was no poison involved Benson knew that. Do you suppose Benson would have left his sampler in his laboratory smeared with poison as evidence against himself? Do you suppose he kept any poison where it might be found by accident?"

"But the poison on the pellet."

". . . was simple gelatin, unflavored. Benson would have known it would be something like that. That's why the Space Ranger did not try to get a confession out of him. That's why he had him gagged, to prevent a warning. Hennes might have figured it out for himself, if he hadn't been in blind panic."

"Well, I'll be tossed out into Space," said Dr. Silvers blankly.

He was still rubbing his chin when he finally made his excuses and went off to bed.

David turned to Bigman.

"And what will you be doing now, Bigman?"

Bigman said, "Dr. Silvers has offered me a permanent job with the Council. But I don't think I'll take it."

"Why not?"

"Well, I'll tell you, Mr. Starr. I sort of figure on going with you, wherever you happen to be going after this."

"I'm just going to Earth," said David.

They were alone, yet Bigman looked cautiously over his shoulder before he spoke. "It seems to me you'll be going lots of places besides Earth—Space Ranger."

"*What?*"

185

"Sure. I knew that when I first saw you come in with all that light and smoke. That's why I didn't take you serious when it looked as if you were accusing me of being the poisoner." His face was broken out in a giant grin.

"Do you know what you're talking about?"

"I sure do. I couldn't see your face, or the details of your costume, but you were wearing hip boots and you were the right height and build."

"Coincidence."

"Maybe. I couldn't see the design on the hip boots but I made out a little of them, the colors, for instance. And you're the only farmboy I ever heard of that was willing to wear simple black and white."

David Starr threw his head back and laughed. "You win. Do you really want to join forces with me?"

"I'd be proud to," said Bigman.

David held out his hand and the two shook.

"Together then," said David, "wherever we go."